Somehow, Greg Clayton had bonded with the baby.

Why else would he always be asking about her, always checking on her?

When Greg didn't return right away, Connie made her way to the bedroom to peek in on them, and what she saw caused her heart to melt.

There sat Greg in the rocker, the tiny newborn cradled on his chest. The pink flannel receiving blanket had come unwrapped, and one little bootie had slipped out. He was humming a tune she hadn't heard before, and when he glanced up at her, when their eyes met...

So much for pretending there wasn't anything going on between them.

D0039722

Dear Reader,

Her Best Christmas Ever takes place during my favorite time of the year and concludes on Christmas Day at the Rocking C Ranch. If you like to read about cowboys, babies and country music, you're going to enjoy this story, which is the third and last book in THE TEXAS HOMECOMING series.

I don't know about you, but I love the holiday season. There's a sense of hope and wonder that fills the winter air. And it's a perfect time to count our many blessings.

As you ponder the perfect gifts for friends and loved ones, consider giving yourself a special gift this month by reaching out to someone less fortunate. Your church, synagogue or favorite community service organization can provide you with many ideas, one of which just might touch your heart.

Wishing you and yours a wonderful holiday filled with unexpected blessings,

Judy

HER BEST
CHRISTMAS EVER

JUDY DUARTE

Silhouette®

SPECIAL EDITION®

Published by Silhouette Books

America's Publisher of Contemporary Romance

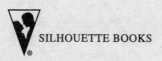

SILHOUETTE BOOKS

ISBN-13: 978-0-373-24943-5
ISBN-10:   0-373-24943-8

Recycling programs
for this product may
not exist in your area.

HER BEST CHRISTMAS EVER

Visit Silhouette Books at www.eHarlequin.com

Printed in U.S.A.

Books by Judy Duarte

JUDY DUARTE

always knew there was a book inside her, but since English was her least favorite subject in school, she never considered herself a writer. An avid reader who enjoys a happy ending, Judy couldn't shake the dream of creating a book of her own.

Her dream became a reality in March of 2002, when Silhouette Special Edition released her first book, *Cowboy Courage*. Since then, she has sold twenty-one more novels.

Her stories have touched the hearts of readers around the world. In July of 2005, Judy won the prestigious Readers' Choice Award for *The Rich Man's Son*.

Judy makes her home near the beach in Southern California. When she's not cooped up in her writing cave, she's spending time with her somewhat enormous but delightfully close family.

You can write to Judy c/o Silhouette Books, 233 Broadway, Suite 1001, New York, NY 10237. You can also contact her at JudyDuarte@sbcglobal.net or through her Web site, www.judyduarte.com.

To Crystal Green and Sheri WhiteFeather,
the best critique partners in the world.
I have no idea where I'd be
or what I'd do without you two in my corner.

Chapter One

Hoping to beat the storm that darkened the vast Texas sky, Greg Clayton stepped harder on the gas pedal, accelerating the rental SUV.

He'd just wrapped up another grueling tour, and the members of his country-western band had scattered, each one going his or her own way for the upcoming holiday season. Greg had boarded a flight, too, and was now heading for the only place he'd ever really called home—the Rocking C.

Fourteen years ago, Granny Clayton had found him hiding in her barn, alone and afraid. Within a month, she'd started adoption proceedings to make him a part of her family.

And now, at twenty-seven, he'd been a Clayton half his life—the *best* half by far.

A jagged streak of lightning ripped through the clouds, which were growing more ominous by the minute, and it didn't take long for a groan and rumble of thunder to follow.

Greg swore under his breath. This storm—the first of two, if the weatherman had called it right—was going to be a real gully-washer.

Fortunately, he wasn't far from the ranch. But there was one particular dip in the county road that was prone to flooding with any significant precipitation, so he needed to get past that low spot before the rain began to fall. Otherwise, he wouldn't be able to get through at all.

When his cell phone rang, he grabbed it off the clip on his belt and answered.

"Greg?" his elderly mother asked over the crackling line. "Is that you?"

"Yes. Is everything okay, Granny?"

"Well, yes and no. *I'm* doing fine, but I'm afraid Lester had a stroke. He was visiting his sister in Houston when it happened."

"That's too bad." Lester was Granny's foreman, a position he'd stepped in to fill after Clem Bixby died. As far as the ranch went, Lester did a great job. But no one would ever replace Clem when it came to having a positive, paternal influence on three adolescent boys.

"Where are you?" Greg asked, scanning the ominous, charcoal-gray horizon and hoping she was close to her destination. He didn't like the idea of her being out on the road, especially at her age.

"I'm with Hilda," she said. "So you don't need to worry about me."

Greg rolled his eyes in a silent scoff. That was supposed to make him feel better? While Hilda was only a couple of years younger than Granny, she seemed to be the designated driver these days. And more often than not, the two tended to get into trouble when they were together.

Not that the women drank; they were both churchgoing tee-totalers. But together they seemed to get involved in one adventure after another, which gave Greg and his brothers more cause for worry than peace of mind.

"But *where* are you?" he asked.

"Somewhere within Houston city limits," his mother said. "I'm not exactly sure, but we'll be staying in a hotel tonight. It's starting to sprinkle now, so we don't want to be on the streets any more than we have to."

That was a relief.

"How far are you from the ranch?" she asked.

Another flash of lightning struck, followed by a thunderous boom and a celestial shudder. "I'm almost to the county road now, so I'm only a couple of miles from the house."

"Good. The only one left on the ranch is Connie, my cook. Do you remember meeting her?"

Greg had met Connie briefly at Granny's eightieth birthday party in June. The attractive young woman had short brown hair with blond highlights. And she'd baked one heck of a chocolate cake.

If he was lucky, he'd arrive home and find a pot of something tasty simmering on the stove. He hadn't eaten a bite since he'd boarded the plane in Las Vegas. Not that they hadn't served him anything in first class. But he'd been exhausted after the last performance and had slept all the way to Houston's Hobby Airport.

He wouldn't complain, though. He loved being onstage. But sometimes he needed to replenish his creative well, and the best place to do that was at the Rocking C.

So he was looking forward to some downtime and to spending the holidays with the Clayton clan, which was growing. His older brother, Jared, had married Sabrina in a quiet little ceremony a couple of months ago. And Matt was now engaged to Tori.

Yep. Greg would enjoy catching up with his brothers and the new ladies in their lives.

Of course, by the time New Year's Eve rolled around, he'd be ready to meet up with the band and begin the winter tour.

"I gave all of the ranch employees time off for Thanksgiving," Granny said, drawing Greg back to the conversation they'd been having. "But Connie didn't want to travel. So when I got the call about Lester's stroke, I had to leave her all by herself, which I really didn't want to do. So I'm sure glad to know you'll be with her, especially since there's a storm brewing."

"No problem. I'll keep her company." Greg found himself smiling. To be honest, he was looking forward to seeing Connie again. She'd been pretty quiet when they'd been introduced five months ago, and her shyness or disinterest or whatever it had been had intrigued him.

Most women, whether they were young or old, single or attached, seemed to fawn over Greg, so he was looking forward to doing some of the chasing for a change.

After disconnecting the line, he continued to the ranch, arriving about five minutes after the first sprinkle of rain hit his windshield. He parked close to the house and entered through the back door, where he removed his hat and boots and left them in the mudroom.

Just inside the kitchen, he caught the aroma of warm cinnamon and spice, and his stomach growled in response.

Since he figured his mother had told Connie he was coming, he didn't announce his arrival. Instead, he walked into the living room, where he found her snoozing on the sofa. In her arms, she cuddled a pillow. She'd draped an autumn-colored afghan over her and had it pulled up to her chin.

Her hair was longer now; the blond highlights were gone. He couldn't decide whether he liked it that way or not. Still, she was just as pretty as he remembered. Her face, with its light olive-colored complexion, practically glowed.

If his memory hadn't failed him, her eyes were a greenish shade of hazel. Of course, he'd have to wait until they opened to know for sure.

A grin stretched across his face. Something told him he was going to really enjoy this particular visit home. And he almost looked forward to a fire in the hearth and the sound of rain on the roof.

Realizing he couldn't continue to stand there and stare at her, he decided to let her sleep and to carry his luggage into his room. But as he took a step, one of the slats of hardwood flooring squeaked in protest.

Connie gasped and shot up on the sofa, her eyes—yep, definitely green—growing wide.

"Oops," Greg said, placing his bag on the floor. "I didn't mean to scare you."

Her mouth opened, yet she didn't attempt to speak, so he

added, "I'm Greg. Granny's son. We met at her birthday party a few months back."

"I know who you are," she said, running her hand through her brown locks of hair. She didn't seem to be impressed.

"I thought I'd put my bags away," Greg said, "then fix myself something to eat."

"I can do it." She threw off the pillow, as well as the afghan, revealing a belly the size of a basketball. No, make that a beach ball.

Damn. She was *pregnant*.

The absolute shock must have shown on his face, because she rubbed her distended womb, furrowed her brow, and asked, "What's the matter?"

"You…" He shrugged. "You're going to have a baby."

"Didn't you know?"

"Nope." And no one had told him. Not his mother, his brothers…. How could they neglect to mention something like that? He didn't think that he'd kept his attraction to her a secret.

Lightning cracked across the sky, briefly illuminating the room.

No wonder Granny had worried about leaving Connie home alone. She looked ready to…pop.

"When are you due?" he asked, hoping it was a month or two from now. Hell, even next week would give him some peace of mind.

"On Friday," she said.

And this was Tuesday. He hoped that the kid would stay on schedule.

Connie rubbed the small of her back and grimaced.

"What's the matter?" he asked.

She arched, all the while continuing her massage. "I've had a backache all afternoon."

He glanced at the antique clock on the mantel. Five-fifteen.

For a man who'd been looking forward to having some time alone with a woman and turning on the charm, he'd sure changed his tune. Now all he could think about was making it through the night and hoping Granny wouldn't decide to spend any extra time in Houston.

"I'll get you something to eat while you put away your things," she said.

"No, I can't let you do that, especially since you're hurting. Go ahead and lie down again. I'll just make a sandwich. In fact, I'll make two—one for each of us."

"Well," she said, "as long as it's no trouble…."

"It's not." And that was the absolute truth. Hell, he needed to keep his hands busy and his thoughts on something else.

Otherwise, he was going to spend the next umpteen hours stressed out of his ever-lovin' mind.

Connie's back had been aching like crazy, but it had seemed to ease some over the last hour. Her heart was still skipping and jumping all over the place, though.

She'd been sound asleep when Greg had entered the house. And while she'd known he was coming, she hadn't been expecting him until later this evening.

I'm Greg, he'd said. *Granny's son. We met at her birthday party a few months back.*

Connie hadn't needed the introduction. She'd known exactly

who the tall, dark-haired man was. His handsome face had adorned the covers of several of her favorite CDs, and his voice had been a regular on KCOW, the radio station she'd always listened to when she'd lived near Galveston.

In fact, Greg might never understand why, but when she realized that her employer's son was *the* Greg Clayton whose hits were tearing up the charts, Connie had nearly given two weeks notice and begun looking for a new job.

Not that Greg would have any idea who *she* was. Her singing career, as short-lived as it was, had been limited to gigs at seedy, two-bit bars. It had also been a surreal time in her life she wanted to forget.

After Ross's last drunken rage, Connie had made up her mind that she wouldn't ever let him hit her again. That she was going to make some changes in her life. Some big ones.

"Do you want to press charges?" the first officer on the scene that night had asked, as his partner called for an ambulance.

She'd nodded. "Yes, I do."

The violence had started as a push here and a shove there. Over time, it had escalated to a twist of her arm, which had been so hard that she'd thought he might have broken something. At that point, she'd told herself she wouldn't tolerate any more rough stuff.

The first time he actually struck her and split open her lip, he'd cried like a baby and been so remorseful that she'd softened and gone against her best judgement.

"I'm sorry, baby," he'd said. "I just love you *so* much." Then he'd apologized and promised it would never happen again.

It was a promise he hadn't been able to keep.

Connie hadn't grown up in a violent home, so the next time he'd blown up had been the last. She'd refused to live with a bully any longer.

As the officer read him his rights, Ross had grown even angrier. While being helped into the back of the patrol car, he'd yelled to Connie, "You're going to be sorry for this."

She'd been sorry already. Sorry for getting involved with him in the first place, sorry she hadn't left him the very first time he'd raised his voice and had given her a shove.

A rumble of thunder sounded in the distance, drawing her from the dark memories, and she padded to the window to peer out into the rain.

Her mother always said that this kind of day called for a pot of soup and homemade bread.

Connie agreed, even if she wasn't all that good at whipping anything up in the kitchen that wasn't a dessert. She was getting better at fixing meals, though, thanks to Granny's insistence that she do the bulk of the cooking in spite of her limited experience.

"You've got to learn sometime," the older woman had said, "especially since you're going to be a mother in a few short months."

Connie blew out a sigh and rubbed the small of her back, which had begun to ache all over again.

Had she done too much or pulled something? Or was this just one of the many discomforts associated with the last weeks of pregnancy?

For a moment, she wondered if she might be going into labor. After all, the books she'd read mentioned something about a backache. But it seemed as though she'd been plagued with a similar pain off and on for the past few days or so.

She had a doctor's appointment tomorrow, so she'd have to ask about it. Especially since it seemed to be hurting worse today than before.

Maybe sleeping on the soft sofa hadn't been good for her.

Thinking that it might be better if she moved around a bit, she headed to the kitchen where Greg was fixing sandwiches for them.

Earlier, she'd baked a cake, but she'd put off preparing anything else to eat until after she'd taken a nap, which made her feel somewhat remiss now. She'd been hired to cook the meals, so she didn't want anyone to think she was slacking off. Neither did she want anyone to think that her pregnancy—or the baby— would hamper her ability to work and pull her own weight. She needed this job and a safe, out-of-the-way place to live.

As she stepped into the doorway, she found Greg standing at the counter, his long, dark hair pulled back with a strip of leather and hanging past his broad shoulders.

He was loading up slices of bread in Dagwood style, with ham, turkey, cheese, sliced tomatoes and whatever else he'd been able to find by rummaging in the fridge.

It was strange to see someone of his caliber standing so close, to see a talented, sexy man engaged in a run-of-the-mill task. He appeared to be one part cowboy, one part warrior, and she found herself in awe.

But she was determined not to fawn over him like a starstruck groupie.

"How about a piece of apple-spice cake?" she asked, shrugging off any misplaced attraction as she entered the kitchen.

"Sure, I've got a real sweet tooth, so that sounds great." He glanced over his shoulder and tossed her his trademark smile, which did a real number on her hormones. And not the maternal kind.

Weird, she thought. Even nine months pregnant, with her thoughts and her body focused on a new baby and upcoming childbirth, she was still flattered by his attention in a male/female sort of way. But she did her best to ignore it and went to work.

After cutting two pieces of cake—one large and one small— she placed them on dessert plates.

"Let's eat in the living room," Greg said. "It's getting chilly, and I want to start a fire. Besides, you'll probably be more comfortable in there."

He was right about that.

Ten minutes later, as several flames licked the logs Greg had stacked in the hearth, Connie reached for the afghan, wrapping it around her and the baby that slept in her womb. She'd decided to call her daughter Amanda, after a friend she'd once had, a neighbor girl who'd moved away the same summer Connie's daddy had died.

It had been a cruel blow, a double whammy for a ten-year-old. And, for a while, she'd wondered if she could handle the heartbreak, the loneliness.

Eventually, the incredible sadness became bearable, but the loneliness never went away.

Outside the wind howled, and the rain came down in a steady sheet. Connie never had liked the wind. Not since watching *The Wizard of Oz* and hearing about Texas twisters that had wreaked havoc on entire cities.

"Do you have family?" Greg asked.

She turned her head, saw him watching her from across the sofa. "Yes. A mom and a sister."

"Do they live around here?"

"Not too far." She didn't particularly want to talk about them. She'd never been a good liar, and since the truth hurt, she preferred to change the subject whenever possible.

"Granny said you didn't want to take time off for the holiday."

"I thought it might be best to stick close to my doctor in Brighton Valley."

"You mean Doc Graham?" Greg asked. "He's the only one in town, as far as I know."

"Actually, Doc retired a couple of months back, and Dr. Bramblett took over his practice."

"Are you okay with that?" Greg asked. "I know Doc is getting on in years. And most doctors his age would have retired a decade or more ago. But he's got a solid reputation for having a good bedside manner and being a top-notch diagnostician, at least as far as small-town physicians go."

"I know what you mean. And, yes, I was a little disappointed when he introduced me to Dr. Bramblett. But I really like her, too. It'll be okay."

Both doctors had assured her that she was healthy and that they had no reason to believe she'd have any problems. In fact, during her last exam, Dr. Bramblett had said that the baby was in perfect position—head down and dropped low in the pelvis.

Still, Connie had to admit she was a little nervous and scared about actually having the baby, even if she'd read everything she could get her hands on lately.

"Is your mother going to be with you for the birth?" Greg asked.

"No, I don't think so." In truth, Connie hadn't told her mom or her sister that she was expecting. Neither of them had approved of Ross, even though they hadn't known he had a drinking problem and was abusive.

Her mother had been relieved to know that he and Connie had broken up for good, but she wouldn't be the least bit happy to learn her youngest daughter was going to be an unwed mother.

A small part of Connie was tempted to tuck her tail between her legs and run home to Mama anyway, but she just couldn't bring herself to do that. Her mother—Dinah Rawlings of daytime television fame—had a conservative audience and wouldn't appreciate the bad publicity right now, even if Connie's days of rebellion were over.

Besides, ever since her father's death, it seemed that their mother/daughter relationship had been steadily deteriorating. Now it was more of a facade than anything.

In part, Connie blamed her mother's obsession with work and those stupid television ratings for the rift. But she knew it went much deeper than that. She'd never been able to compete with her older sister.

Yet even if she and her mom got along great, she was afraid Ross might be able to find her through her mother. And Connie couldn't let him do that.

Nor could she risk letting him learn they'd conceived a baby during their tumultuous time together. Ross had lost his temper more than once, making Connie the victim of domestic violence.

What might he do to a child?

* * *

The evening, as awkward as it promised to be, stretched before them like a bungee cord pulled to its limit, ready to bounce or snap at any moment. So Greg turned on the television, which seemed to help. At least, the men's action flick he'd settled on had made the time pass. If Connie didn't like the movie he'd chosen, she didn't mention it.

But just before eight, when the villain was about to get his comeuppance, the power went out, causing the television to shut down with a whoosh and the house to go dark.

The only light came from the fireplace, which was still going strong.

"Uh-oh." Connie's voice bore the hint of a tremble.

"Don't worry." Greg pushed himself out of the leather recliner on which he'd been sitting and stood. Then he made his way to the hearth, where he took the candles from a grouping on the mantel and stooped to hold the wicks—one at a time—near the flame until they lit. When he was finished, he placed the candles throughout the room.

He wondered if Granny still kept the flashlights in the mudroom. Probably. He would just have to carry a candle with him when he went to look.

After he'd finished creating a bit more illumination in the room, he turned to find that Connie had pulled the afghan closer, nearly to her chin, as though hiding behind it.

"There isn't anything to be afraid of," he said.

"I never have liked to be alone in a storm."

"Hey." He chuckled, trying to make light of it. "You're not alone. You've got me."

For the first time this evening, she smiled. The warmth in her eyes made her appear even prettier than before.

When he'd first been introduced to her, he'd been told her last name was Montoya. He'd assumed she'd had Latino blood, like him. Yet she was fairer than he was.

"You ought to smile more often," he said. But he didn't see any reason to tell her why.

"There hasn't been much to be happy about in the past year or so."

He waited for her to explain, but she didn't, and he was torn between letting the subject die and trying to revive it. But without the television or radio to distract him, all he could think about was the pregnant woman sitting next to him.

"Are you unhappy about having a baby?" he finally asked.

She caressed the basketball-size mound of her belly. "The timing certainly could have been better. But it's not her fault."

"Her?"

"I'm having a little girl." Connie smiled again, which gave him a sense of relief. "At least, that's what Dr. Bramblett said during my ultrasound."

Greg wasn't often reminded of the woman who'd given birth to him. She'd died the day he was born, and he'd never had the chance to meet her. But his *tia*, his aunt, had told him how his mother used to sing to him while he was inside her womb. How determined she'd been to provide him with a happy home and a future.

Eventually, he'd been blessed with the things his mother had wanted for him, but she'd never lived to see it or to be a part of it. And that made him sad—sad for her because she would never know how hard he'd tried to make her proud.

Did Connie think about her baby like that? Did she have hopes and plans for her child's future? Had the baby become real to her?

Somehow, the answer seemed to matter more than it should.

"What are you going to name your daughter?" he asked.

"I'm leaning toward Amanda. But I suppose I'll have to see what she looks like. Something else, like Megan or Tricia, might be more fitting."

That made sense, he supposed.

He had no idea what his mother would have named him, had she lived. His aunt had been the one to choose Gregorio, after the priest who'd delivered him.

Greg and Connie each fell into silence. Lost in their own thoughts, he supposed.

The candles cast a soft glow in the room, and the flames caressed the logs in the hearth. The crackling embers struck up an interesting harmony with the rain pounding on the window panes, creating an aura that would have been romantic if Connie hadn't been expecting a baby.

"Will you be staying on at the ranch after she's born?" he asked.

"I plan to. Brighton Valley seems like a good place to raise a family."

"Maybe," Greg said. "But I'd get cabin fever if I were stuck in a place like this for very long."

"With your career, I guess it's a good thing you like traveling."

"Yes, I do. I suspect you're a real homebody, though."

"More so now than ever." She tossed him another smile, and it touched a chord deep in his heart. "After the mess I got myself into, I'm looking forward to a quiet, peaceful life."

"What mess was that?" Greg didn't usually quiz people, so his knee-jerk curiosity surprised him. But he couldn't help wondering about Connie's past, about what had brought her to the Rocking C.

She stroked her belly. "Let's just say I didn't plan on getting pregnant."

"I take it that you and the father aren't together anymore." Greg watched her expression, trying to read into each twitch of the eye, each faint movement of her lips.

"Getting involved with that man was the biggest mistake I ever made," she admitted.

"Does he know about the baby?"

"No. And he won't ever know about her if I can help it."

There was only one conclusion for him to make. "The guy must have been a real jerk."

She fingered the crocheted edge of the afghan, then looked up at him. "He was mean and jealous whenever he drank. And toward the end, that seemed to be all he ever did."

Greg had known his share of men like that. And while he thought about quizzing her further, he figured some memories were best left alone.

They made small talk for a while, nothing personal. And as the antique clock on the mantel gonged for the ninth time, Connie yawned.

"You know," she said, struggling to balance the bulk of her girth as she got to her feet, "I'm winding down faster than that clock. I think I'd better go to bed."

"All right. Sleep tight." He watched her go, thinking that she didn't look the least bit pregnant from behind.

But Connie didn't get five steps away when she froze in her

steps and looked down at the floor, where a puddle of water pooled at her feet.

As her gaze met Greg's, she seemed to silently ask, "What should I do?"

And he'd be damned if he knew.

Chapter Two

Connie stared down at the floor, as though she could blink her eyes and find that she'd only imagined that her water had broken.

But it had; her legs and slacks were wet with the warm fluid.

Of all days and nights for this to happen. She slid a glance at Greg, saw the shock plastered on his face, matching her own.

Fear gripped her throat. This couldn't be happening. The backache that had been plaguing her all afternoon sharpened to the point of taking her breath way. Then it spread around her waist, slicing deep into her womb.

Greg was at her side in an instant, his arm slipping around her. "Are you okay?"

"I… I don't know." She leaned into him, needing his support until the pain subsided.

Was she experiencing her first contraction?

She must be.

Focus, she told herself, as she quickly tried to sort through the instructions her doctor had given her, as well as the information she'd gleaned from the book she'd read on what to expect during pregnancy and childbirth.

Finally, the pain eased completely, and she slowly straightened. "I've got to call Dr. Bramblett. She'll know what to do."

"Good idea." Greg handed her his cell phone.

"And I guess I'd better clean up this mess," she said.

"I'll take care of that. You just call the doctor and sit down. If that happens again, you might collapse and hurt something."

"I…" She nodded at the amniotic fluid on the floor. "Maybe you'd better get me something to sit on. I don't want to ruin any of your mother's chairs."

She could have sworn she heard him swear under his breath as he dashed off to get what she'd requested.

When he left the room, she dialed the doctor's number from memory. But instead of one of the familiar, friendly voices she expected to hear, a woman who worked for the answering service took the call.

"Dr. Bramblett is out of town," the woman reported. "But Doc Graham is covering for her."

That meant the older man would deliver her baby, and in a sense she was almost relieved. Doc Graham might be past retirement age, but he'd gained a tremendous amount of experience during his fifty-year practice.

When Doc's voice finally sounded over the line, she said, "This is Connie Montoya, and my water just broke."

"Where are you?" he asked. "Are you at the Rocking C?"

"Yes, I am." Doc was in Brighton Valley, which was about ten minutes away. And the hospital in Wexler was about thirty miles beyond that. He'd probably tell her to grab her bag and come right away.

Instead, he said, "I'm afraid there's no way you or anyone else can get in or out of there right now because of the flooding."

Had she imagined a raw edge to his grandfatherly voice? A tinge of fear?

Her heart dropped to the pit of her stomach, and her voice took on high-pitched tone. "What am I going to do?"

"Don't worry. Usually, once the rain stops for a while, the county road opens up again."

She wanted to believe him, but it was a real struggle. She placed a hand on her womb as though she could convince the baby to stay inside and wait for a more convenient time to arrive.

"The weather report says that the rains are supposed to start easing by midnight," Doc added, "and it won't take long for the road to open up after that. So you should be okay until then."

Should be? But what if she wasn't? What if the baby needed medical intervention? Or what if she did?

"Can an ambulance get through?" Connie asked. "Or maybe you can send a helicopter." Somehow, she had to get to a hospital.

"I'm afraid not. The ambulance can't make it any sooner than I can. And the chopper can't take off right now. But in a couple of hours…"

"Hours?" Connie asked.

"Edna's an old hand at this," Doc said. "She's helped me deliver a few babies over the years. So if worse comes to worst, you'll be in good hands."

"But Granny isn't *here*." Connie's voice had risen a couple of decibels and was bordering on sheer panic.

"Who's with you?" Doc asked. "You're not alone, are you?"

Connie slid a glance at Greg, watching as he came into the family room and dropped a towel onto the floor to dry up the fluid.

"No," she told the doctor. "I'm not alone. Greg's with me."

"Good. He's been raised around cattle and horses. He'll know what to do if it comes to that."

What did he mean by "if it comes to that"?

Was he suggesting that a country singer be her midwife? And not just any singer, but the one and only Greg Clayton?

She blew out a sigh. Greg had been raised around cattle and horses, Doc had said. Was that supposed to make Connie feel better?

She didn't care if the guy had a degree in veterinary medicine. She wanted a *doctor*—*her* doctor. And she wanted to have her baby in a hospital.

After giving her a few do's and don'ts, Doc added, "As soon as the rainfall stops and the water recedes, I'll drive out to the ranch. If the weatherman was right and this storm strikes hard and quick, I should be able to get through that road before dawn."

Connie glanced out the window, where the rain continued to pound as though it would never end.

"For what it's worth," Doc added, "first babies usually take their time being born. You have hours to go. In fact, you probably won't even deliver until tomorrow night."

She hoped he was right. If anyone had a handle on this sort of thing it was Doc.

But that didn't make Connie feel any better about being stuck out on the ranch without a physician—or even a veterinarian.

What was Greg going to do—sing the baby a lullaby?

Greg had never been so scared in his entire life. And that was saying a lot.

Before he'd moved in with Granny, he'd had plenty of reasons to be afraid. Like being left at a Mexican orphanage when he was six years old. And going mano a mano with a furious, unbalanced, thirty-something migrant worker when Greg had been only thirteen.

Now, as he sat in Connie's bedroom with every candle and flashlight he could find glowing, it seemed as though he was even more out of his element than he'd ever been before.

It was just after midnight, and he'd been planted in a chair beside her bed for three hours, afraid to leave her alone—even to take a bathroom break.

Her pain had grown progressively worse. But at least she hadn't cried out, which would have really wrung the ice-cold sweat out of him.

After another brutal contraction eased, she seemed to regroup. So he took the wet cloth he'd been using to wipe her brow, dipped it into a bowl of cool water, then dabbed it across her forehead.

He didn't know if that was helping or not, but he'd seen someone do that in a movie once. And he wanted to do *something,* even if he felt about as useful as a sow bug on the underside of a rock.

"How are you doing?" he asked.

"Not bad when I'm between contractions," she said, obviously attempting to make light of all of this.

His best guess was that her pains were lasting nearly two minutes, and her reprieve wasn't even that long. But he had to give her credit for not screaming. He'd really be in a fix then. His nerves, which he'd once thought were like cords of steel, reminded him of cooked spaghetti noodles now.

"According to Doc Graham," she said, "first babies take hours to be born. And he should be here by the time we need him."

"That's good to know." Greg wondered who she was trying to make feel better—him or her. It didn't matter, he supposed. Either way, they were in this mess together.

And what a mess it was. Talk about being at a loss and completely out of his comfort zone.

Greg had watched his share of births on the ranch, but they'd all been animals. He glanced down at Connie, at the grimace on her face, and his fear deepened.

What if something went wrong? What if he didn't know what to do or how to help her?

He did his best to tamp down the concern and worry, as they continued to ride out the storm—the one raging outside, as well as the one going on in her body.

Finally, just after one o'clock, she turned her head toward him. Pain clouded her eyes.

As she wrapped her gaze around his, threatening to pull him under as he dog-paddled around in a sea of his own anxiety, she reached for him and locked her fingers around his forearm. "Will the road be closed much longer?"

"The rain has really let up, so the water should start receding as soon as the downpour stops completely."

"This is getting to be unbearable," she said. "So I hope you're right."

Greg hoped so, too.

What if something went wrong—like it had the night he was born?

His biological mother, Maria Vasquez, had been nearly nine months pregnant and living in Mexico when she'd decided to return to the United States to have her baby. She'd been born in Houston, but after the death of her parents, she'd moved back to Mexico to live with an older sister. And since Greg's father had been a drifter who hadn't been willing to marry her or accept responsibility for the child he'd helped create, she knew she was on her own.

Maria had been a dreamer, while her sister Guadalupe had never been one to take risks. But Maria knew having U.S. citizenship, like she had, would provide her child advantages he wouldn't have in Mexico. So she managed to finally talk Guadalupe into leaving the small village where they lived and going to Texas with her.

Unfortunately, they'd no more than crossed the border when Maria's water broke, and she went into labor.

They'd tried to reach Houston, but her labor progressed too quickly. So they'd decided to stop at the very next town they came to. But by that time, it was late at night, and there was nothing open—no gas station, no motel, no diner…

When they spotted a small church, Guadalupe stopped the car and banged on the door until a priest answered. He'd called an ambulance and done his best to make Maria comfortable, but medical help didn't arrive in time. Maria died from complications of childbirth and was later buried in the church cemetery.

The thought of history repeating itself scared the crap out of

Greg. Focusing on the past, on the stories that Tia Guadalupe had told him, only served to increase his anxiety now.

He'd never considered himself a religious person, even if he'd been named Gregorio, after the kindly priest. But he prayed anyway, asking that the rain would let up soon and that the doctor would be able to get to the Rocking C in time.

Doc might have said that first babies took hours to be born, but Greg feared that Connie's baby might not be aware of that rule.

"Oh, my God." As the overwhelming urge to push overtook her, Connie looked at Greg, the only person in the world who could help her now.

But as their eyes met, she couldn't utter another word, couldn't tell him what was going on. All she could do was instinctively tighten her stomach and curl up, as a half groan/half growl erupted from her lips.

"What's wrong?" he asked, no longer even trying to mask the concern in his voice.

Poor Greg. He was as frightened as Connie was—maybe more so.

And she was scared to death.

But there wasn't anything she could do right now, other than obey the primal urging of her body to push the baby out into the world.

Finally, between grunts and groans and other horrid noises that would have been mortifying if she'd made them at any other time, Connie managed to squeak out, "The...baby's... coming."

"No!" Greg leaned forward, his eyes growing wide enough

to allow the panic inside of him to peer out. "Don't push yet, Connie. Can't you try to wait just a little—"

"Are you crazy?" she shrieked. "Get out of here and leave me alone!"

When he stood, she yelled, "Please don't go!"

"God, Connie, I won't. I just thought I should boil water or something. Or at least wash my hands." Greg raked his fingers through his hair as though forgetting that the strands were being held taut by a leather queue.

The poor guy. She almost felt sorry for him, for the distress her labor was putting him through. But only *almost*. He was all she had right now, and she needed him to step up to the plate.

Of course, this was all her fault. She should have gone home while she'd had the chance. She should have crawled on her hands and knees and begged her mother to forgive her.

But it was too late now.

"Ready or not," she said, "I'm having this baby. And I'm having it *now*."

"Oh, *damn*," he uttered.

Thank goodness he made no effort to leave, even though she could see the anxiety brewing in his eyes.

They were stuck—just the three of them, one man, one woman and one baby. Strangers thrown together by Fate on a lonely, stormy night.

"Oh, God," she whispered. "Don't let my baby die."

Greg paled at her words, and his eyes watered. Then he blinked several times and seemed to rally. "Ah, Connie. Don't worry. I can do this. Hell, so can you. Women have been having babies since the dawn of time. This is no big deal. We'll handle it together. And we'll probably laugh about it later."

No way would she find anything funny about this later. But she appreciated his attempts to calm her, to provide some peace of mind in order to face the challenge ahead. But before she could thank him, her body again took charge, and she heeded another order to push—harder still.

After the urge finally passed, Greg removed the sheet that was covering her legs.

"Take off your panties," Greg said.

"What?" Her expression, she suspected, had morphed into something sort of stupefied. But his comment had struck her as…odd. Under the circumstances, it just…sounded funny, that's all.

"I can't very well deliver the baby if you keep them on," he said patiently.

As Connie worked to remove her underwear—as luck would have it, an extra-large matronly styled pair that Granny had purchased for her—she began to smile. Then a chuckle erupted. One of those nervous, stress-relieving giggles Connie sometimes made at the most unsuitable times and in the most inappropriate places.

"Lucky me," she said. "I wonder how many women can say that Greg Clayton asked her to remove her panties."

"Very funny."

She suspected there had been quite a few—a legion of them, no doubt. She knew how many groupies had flocked around Ross and the other guys who played in the South Forty Band, and they weren't anywhere near as handsome and popular as Greg was.

"Of course," she added, "I suppose this particular experience is unique to the two of us."

"You've got that right." Greg chuffed.

"For what it's worth, after what I've gone through tonight, I can assure you that I won't ever agree to take off my panties for another man again. And if one even suggests it, I'll crack him over the head with the first heavy object I can find."

Greg tossed her a grin. "I'll keep that in mind."

Then he took a deep breath and reached for the cell phone on his belt clip and dialed the number Doc had given him.

"What are you doing?" she asked, feeling the urge to push again.

"Doc is going to have to coach me through this. Like you said, the baby's coming whether we want her to or not."

As Connie pushed until she was blue in the face, she had to agree. Apparently, she was one of those rare women destined for a speedy delivery. And the only one available to help her bring her child into the world was Greg.

She hoped the handsome singer was up for the task.

As Greg prepared to deliver Connie's baby, his movements grew stiff and awkward. The sweat beaded upon his brow, and he used his arm to wipe it away.

Damn. The guys in the band were never going to believe this. Hell, *he* didn't believe it. If his hands weren't busy, he'd pinch himself.

His cell phone was lying beside him, set on speaker, as Doc Graham talked him through the scariest, most nerve-racking night of his life.

He glanced at Connie, her expression set in a grimace, her face red as she did her best to push her baby into the world.

Was this how Father Gregorio felt when Greg's mother had been giving birth? Scared spitless? Completely out of his league?

The fact that his mom had died in childbirth was enough to spike his spinal fluid with ice water, but he shook off the nervous fear and focused on the task at hand. He had to help Connie have her baby whether he wanted to or not.

"The head is out," Greg told both Doc and Connie, as he followed the directions of the experienced country doctor.

Moments later, the baby slid into his hands. His own breath held as he waited for it to cry, to breathe. As the tiny little girl let out a wail that pierced the silence and announced her arrival, he blew out a huge sigh of relief.

His movements were almost robotic, but he did everything Doc told him to do, step by scary step. And as the minutes ticked away, as everything proceeded the way Doc said that it would, wonder overcame the fear that had been dogging him since Connie's labor had started and the birth became imminent.

After he cleaned up the screaming, flailing baby girl, he bundled her in flannel like a little burrito and handed her to her mother.

Connie, with tears streaming down her face, took the baby from him and cooed at her. "Hello, sweetheart. Welcome to the world."

A sense of awe washed over Greg, and he found himself experiencing an unprecedented high, a mind-boggling sense of wonder.

"Oh, my God." Connie looked up from the newborn long enough to latch onto Greg's gaze. "Look at her."

He had been looking. And while the tiny little newborn was scrawny and wrinkly and gooey and had an uncanny resemblance to E.T., the extra-terrestrial, he couldn't help thinking she was the cutest little alien he'd ever seen.

"She's beautiful," he told Connie. "Are you still going to call her Amanda?"

"I don't know. Does she look like an Isabella to you?"

She was asking *him* for an opinion? "It sounds like an awfully big name for a little baby, but I guess she'll grow into it."

"I could nickname her Bella. Or Izzy."

Greg looked at the little flannel-wrapped cherub, at the rosebud mouth, the wispy dark hair.

"Not Izzy," he said, thinking of a ton of rhyming words that kids might use to tease her, *Dizzy* or *Frizzy* or *Lizzy Lizard*. Kids could be thoughtless, he'd learned. And cruel. "But Belle or Bella suits her. Either one would make a good name for a little princess."

Then he tore his gaze away from the mother and child, doing whatever he could to make Connie more comfortable.

Yet even when his job appeared to be nearly over, when he finally had an excuse to close the door and leave them to rest, he hadn't been able to do so. Instead, he kept looking for reasons to stick around.

Had he really been the first human to touch that baby girl? The one to cut and tie the cord?

He sat in silence for the longest time, basking in a slew of emotions he couldn't quite peg. Feelings he'd never experienced, never expected to.

As he got to his feet, he continued to watch them like some

kind of voyeur. Or maybe he'd taken on a protector role. Either way, he couldn't help feeling a bit envious.

Not that he expected to bond with the new little family of two; he'd done his part and could now go on his way. But as Connie whispered loving words to her new daughter, he found her voice soft and mesmerizing, the sight warm and touching.

When the baby looked at her with eyes that crossed, Greg damn near choked up. Again, he wondered if he really ought to be privy to this special moment, yet he was unable to move.

Awed by what he'd just seen, he was also caught up in admiration for the woman who'd bravely fought pain and fear to bring her newborn daughter into the world, a woman who now bore a maternal glow and a mesmerizing beauty he couldn't explain.

Connie, who cuddled her infant daughter in her arms, looked up at him and smiled. "Thank you, Greg. I don't know what I would have done without you here."

"It was no big deal," he said.

But it had been bigger than big. It had been *huge*.

He didn't think he'd ever forget this moment. He'd witnessed a miracle, and what had once seemed like the worst night of his life had somehow become one of the best.

The kind of night that made a musician want to grab his guitar and sit up until dawn, trying to re-create a memory in song.

Chapter Three

The telephone rang shortly before daybreak, and Greg snatched it from its cradle so the noise wouldn't wake Connie or the baby.

They were both resting now, and he wanted to keep it that way. Connie had been through hell the past couple of hours and a peaceful rest had been well earned.

"Hello?" he whispered into the receiver.

The age-worn voice boomed over the line. "It's Doc Graham. How's our patient doing?"

"Okay. She and the baby are both asleep."

Of course, that in itself didn't mean that everything was fine, which was why Greg kept checking in on them every few minutes. He wanted to make sure they were still breathing and that their coloring was good.

"But I'll sure feel better when you get here," he told the doctor. "Then you can validate my diagnosis."

"It won't be long," Doc said. "I've just driven past that low spot in the road and should be at the ranch in about five or ten minutes."

"Good." Knowing Doc the way he did, Greg figured he'd been parked near the flooded area and had driven through the moment he believed it was safe.

"By the way," Doc added, "you did a great job."

Greg didn't know about that. Connie and the baby had done all the work, so he didn't feel right taking credit for the minor role he played. "I didn't do all that much. I'm just thankful there weren't any complications."

"Me, too. How are you holding up, son?"

"All right." Especially now that it was all over.

"I'm sure it's been a long night, so you've got to be tired. As soon as I get there, you can go to bed."

Actually, Greg didn't feel the least bit sleepy. Ever since the baby's birth, he'd had a head-in-the-clouds buzz, one that didn't appear to be fading in the least.

"Well," Doc said over the slightly static telephone line, "I'll see you in a few minutes."

"All right." Greg hung up, but his hand remained on the receiver. For the first time since Connie's water had broken, he finally felt a sense of relief, and it dogged him into the kitchen, where he put on a pot of coffee.

Yet instead of taking a seat or watching out the window for Doc to arrive, he returned to Connie's bedroom and took another peek at her and the baby—just to make sure they were still breathing, that they were resting easy.

And they were.

Connie, her expression softened by something soft and maternal, continued to doze, her head on a fluffy pillow, her brown curls splayed on the white cotton case. She wore no makeup, no sexy clothing, yet Greg was still struck by her beauty.

He'd found her attractive the first day he'd met her, yet there was something even more appealing now.

Maybe it was the strength and bravery she'd shown during the terrible pain she'd endured last night. Or maybe it was something altogether different.

All he knew was that he was inexplicably drawn to her.

She still held the baby next to her, under her arm and close to her heart. They'd called the child Isabella for a while, but for some reason the name didn't seem to fit, and Connie had decided to stick with Amanda, which seemed perfect now.

With tufts of downy black hair, Amanda was a precious little thing. Her head was a bit pointed and misshapen, though.

Greg had asked Doc about it—privately, of course. And he'd been told that it was normal, that it would even out in a few days. He sure hoped so. If it did, he suspected Amanda was going to be the prettiest little girl this side of cherubville.

He leaned against the doorjamb, watching them longer than was necessary. Finally, convinced that an unexpected complication hadn't arisen, he headed to the living room to unlock the door for Doc Graham and to wait on the front porch for his arrival.

Moments later, as he leaned against the wooden railing, watching the pink and orange fingers of dawn stretch across the horizon, he relished the sights and smells of the rain-drenched ranch. At times he missed this place, missed the people who'd become important to him. Yet whenever he came home, he missed the guys in his band, too. The rush of standing onstage. The thrill when he announced a new song he'd written, a song that was met with a roar of approval from the fans.

As Doc Graham's pickup, a red Chevy S-10, pulled into the yard, the front tire struck one of the many puddles that speckled the yard and sent a splatter of dirty water flying.

Greg watched as the old man shut off the ignition, slid out of the driver's seat then reached back for his medical bag.

"Good morning," Greg said.

"It certainly is."

As Greg opened the screen door, Doc wiped his feet on the welcome mat. Once inside the warmth of the house, he shucked off his damp raincoat and left it on the hat tree in the entry.

"So, tell me something," Doc said. "Are you going to turn in your guitar for a stethoscope?"

"No way. But delivering a baby was definitely an experience I won't ever forget." Greg wasn't sure if Doc would understand what he was feeling. After all, in the last half century, Dr. Graham had undoubtedly delivered thousands of babies. So the whole birthing miracle had probably become routine to him.

As Greg led Doc down the hall, he walked lightly so he wouldn't wake Connie or the newborn.

"Well, look who couldn't wait to have her first turkey dinner," Doc said from the doorway of Connie's room.

The new mother's eyes fluttered open, and she blessed the

doctor with a pretty smile. Then she gazed at the baby sleeping in the crook of her arm.

"You know," Doc said, easing closer, "I do believe that's just about the most beautiful newborn I've ever laid eyes on."

Greg watched from the doorway as the doctor examined Connie first. For a moment, Greg wondered whether he should slip out into the living room to allow them some privacy, but he just couldn't seem to turn and walk away.

What if he'd messed up or had forgotten to do something he'd been told to do?

And even if he'd done as good of a job as Doc had told him, he still couldn't help believing that he had some kind of vested interest in both mother and child, although he couldn't quite figure out why.

He hadn't asked for any of this—the storm, the birth—but he'd definitely been sucked in and made an integral, albeit temporary, part of it all. And he wasn't sure when that role would end completely. But until it did, he couldn't bring himself to leave their side for very long.

Nor could he shake the incredible sense of amazement he felt each time he looked at that tiny baby. He'd been part of a miracle tonight, and something told him that his life would never be the same again.

After an initial exam, Doc declared both mother and daughter healthy. "Years ago, I would have just sat down and had a cup of coffee, then promised to come back and check in on you later. But it never hurts to have a second opinion. So, as a precaution, I'm going to send you to the hospital in Wexler and have you both checked out."

That was fine with Greg. He'd be glad for even further validation that everything was okay.

"Are you taking them?" he asked the doctor. "Or should I drive them in myself?"

"Nah," Doc said. "I've lined up an ambulance service to do that. They'll be here in a few minutes. But in the meantime, I could sure use that cup of coffee I was talking about."

"No problem." Greg nodded toward the kitchen. "I just put on a fresh pot."

Moments later, the two men sat at the table with steaming mugs of coffee in front of them. There, Doc answered the questions Greg had about how to care for Connie and the baby once she was discharged from the hospital. He figured Granny would know just what to do, but it was hard to say when she'd get back.

Apparently, now that the hard part was over, there wasn't much more for Greg to do, other than enjoy his coffee and another large serving of the apple-spice cake Connie had made. After cutting two pieces and grabbing a couple of forks, they each dug in.

Dang, that woman could cook.

It was enough to make a man look forward to Thanksgiving dinner—if Connie was the one who was cooking it. But maybe Greg ought to think about calling Caroline down at the diner and asking if he could purchase a take-out turkey dinner.

"Have you been following the news?" Doc asked, as he lifted his fork.

"No. I'm afraid I've been pretty busy the past few hours." Greg took a sip of his coffee, enjoying the rich morning brew. "What's going on?"

"There's another storm coming on the heels of this last one. When it hits, you two might be stranded out here for a while."

As long as Connie and the baby were all right, that didn't bother Greg too much.

"So," Doc added, "if you've got any supplies to stock up on, you'd better do it today. Now that the ground is saturated, the water that fills the low spot in the road won't be as quick to recede."

"I think we're set," Greg said. "Granny's always had a full pantry. But I'll take a look and make sure. When is the next rain supposed to hit?"

"Early tomorrow morning. So it ought to really play havoc with everyone's Thanksgiving plans."

"I wonder if the flights will be delayed," Greg said. "Matt and Tori are supposed to arrive tomorrow from Wyoming. They're on a horse-buying trip."

"That's hard to say." Doc dug into his cake, then closed his eyes as though savoring each chew. "Mmm. This is delicious."

"Connie's a good cook, but since she'll be taking it easy for a while, she's going to be stuck eating whatever I can come up with for meals." Greg chuckled. "I hope she likes canned soup and sandwiches."

They ate in silence, and when they finished, Doc scooted the chair away from the table and got to his feet. "I have to stop by the Tidball place and check on Elmer's big toe. According to Grace, it's been hurting him something fierce."

"What'd he do to it?" Greg asked.

"Elmer swears he didn't do anything. So, if that's the case, it might be gout. From what he said, it sure sounds like it." Doc slid the chair back in place, then ambled across the kitchen and headed toward the front door. "Well, I'd better take off."

"Before the ambulance gets here?" Greg asked.

"Yeah. It'll be here any minute, I suspect. And for what it's worth, it's merely a formality. I doubt the hospital will keep Connie or the baby more than a few hours. They're both doing very well."

Greg hoped so.

He escorted Doc to the door, thanked him, then stood on the porch and watched the white-haired doctor climb into his pickup. When he drove off, Greg returned to Connie's bedroom, where he found her propped up on an elbow and studying Amanda's tiny fingers and toes. She looked up at him, her face glowing almost Madonna-like, and tossed him a smile that darn near squeezed the heart right out of him. "She's absolutely perfect."

Greg grinned. "Yeah. I think so, too."

He leaned against the doorjamb, watching Connie and the baby intently. He'd never known his own mother, but his aunt had told him how much she'd looked forward to his birth and how she'd dreamed that he would make something of his life someday.

Would his mother have held him like Connie was holding Amanda? Would she have marveled at the sight of him, too?

Yeah. She would have.

He couldn't help wishing that she would have lived to see him grow up. To know that he'd become someone people looked up to.

Not that Tia Guadalupe hadn't been a good substitute. But she'd died when he was only six, a loss that had struck him hard and cruel. And with no other family to take him in, he'd been sent to live at the orphanage.

Greg shook off the images and thanked his lucky stars that he'd crossed paths with Granny eventually, that she'd adopted him and made him a part of the ever-growing Clayton family.

Still, while the Rocking C had been the only home he'd known in nearly twenty years, he would never want to live and work here. Not that he minded doing chores and helping out while he was visiting. But he loved the bright lights of the stage and thrived on the fame and the glamour. Whenever he strode out to face the cheering crowds, he knew that he'd finally made it. That he'd finally become the success that his Mama Maria had wanted him to be, that he was living the dream she'd had for him.

"I'd planned to make pies this morning," Connie said, drawing him from his musing. "But that'll have to wait. I might feel more up to baking in the afternoon."

"There's no way you'll be doing anything in the kitchen for a while," he said.

"But Thanksgiving is tomorrow." Connie rose up on the bed. "And everyone is coming here to eat. So I planned—"

"Those plans were changed last night. So don't give Thanksgiving another thought."

"But it's my job—"

"Not *today*. And not tomorrow, either."

She opened her mouth as if to object one more time, and Greg pushed off from the wall, standing straight, his arms still crossed. "Don't make me pull rank on you, ma'am."

"All right." Connie sank back on the bed. "But you might call Sabrina and ask her to help."

"I'm not going to worry about that now."

"Why not?"

"For one thing, it's supposed to rain again, which means Jared and Sabrina might not be able to get through and we might have to postpone the holiday for a day or two. But either way, I can handle it." Of course, only as a last resort. He'd never been too handy in a kitchen. But when he'd been digging through the pantry, he found a bunch of stuff that was pretty easy to make, even for a novice like him.

Connie, who was undoubtedly a great cook, probably wouldn't approve of the simple fare he'd be fixing. He figured that pulling off a major holiday meal probably meant a lot to her.

About the time he was resigning himself to a simple meal, he realized he'd better call the diner in Brighton Valley as soon as it opened and make Caroline, the proprietor, an offer she wouldn't refuse. He'd pay her triple the cost to cook a take-out feast for the Claytons' Thanksgiving, even if he wasn't sure how many of them would show up.

By hook or by crook, they'd have their holiday dinner.

If there was one thing he'd learned since running away from the orphanage and hitching a ride back to Texas when he was thirteen years old, it was that money could buy anything.

Doc had been right. The specialists at the hospital in Wexler had determined that both Connie and the baby were doing great. The resident obstetrician had said they could stay overnight, if she wanted to. But Connie had been eager to get home. With a new storm headed their way, they could get stranded in town, and she wanted to spend Thanksgiving at the ranch.

Greg had seemed a little uneasy about her checking out, but the doctor had assured him that an overnight stay was merely an option. So Greg had relented and brought them both home, using the car seat Connie had been storing in her closet, along with the other new baby things she'd purchased earlier.

Now, as she stood at the bedroom window on Thursday morning and surveyed the clearing skies, she realized that Doc and the weatherman had been wrong. The rain that followed the first storm hadn't struck nearly as hard as predicted. At least, not in Brighton Valley.

Houston, on the other hand, had taken the brunt of the storm. According to Greg, who'd been watching the news as well as the Weather Channel, there were flight delays and travel warnings, so it seemed even more likely that the Clayton family Thanksgiving would be held on Friday or Saturday instead of today.

Connie had planned to go all out with the decorations this year, especially with the candles and the centerpiece, since it would have been her very first attempt to fuss over a holiday the way her mother always did.

But with Amanda's birth and Greg's insistence that she take it easy, she decided to go light this year and do things up big next time around. That is, if she was still living on the Rocking C.

And, of course, there was always Christmas.

Her mother made an even bigger production out of that particular holiday, even though she'd spent more time on the set of *In the Kitchen with Dinah* than she had at home. A habit that Connie had grown to resent.

To be honest, it was nice to use the baby as an excuse not to go home this year. Connie had grown tired of painting on a happy face and pretending that there was nothing she liked better than being in front of a camera for the holidays and pretending to be a member of one of the happiest families in America.

Once upon a time, before Connie's father had died, she had been. Back then, her mother had baked a ton of cookies and goodies, trimmed the hearth and decorated the tree. Even on a shoestring, she'd been able to make their small, two-bedroom house in Houston the best place in the world to be.

But once her mother had taken that job at the television station, everything had changed.

Connie reminded herself that she had a daughter of her own now, a child for whom Connie would create their own family traditions. And if Amanda ever brought home little handmade ornaments and wall hangings and trimmings made out red-and-green construction paper, they would be valued and given their rightful place of honor throughout the house—not set aside for the more lavish, store-bought trinkets.

Family ought to come first.

And now that Amanda was here, Connie vowed to make that a hard-and-fast rule.

When the baby made a gruntlike noise, Connie turned from her vantage point by the window and strode toward the small bassinette. Amanda had begun to squirm and root, a sign that undoubtedly meant she was hungry.

"Hey there, sweet baby." Connie carefully picked up the newborn and placed a kiss upon her cheek. Then she carried her to the rocker, where she took a seat and unbuttoned her nightgown to offer her breast.

As Amanda began to nurse, Connie thought about all that had happened in the past twenty-four hours.

What would she have done the night before last if Greg hadn't been here?

He'd been wonderful, both during the birth and afterward. In fact, he was always popping in to check on her and the baby.

"Hey." His voice sounded from the doorway again. "Oops. Sorry."

She glanced up, realizing he'd spotted her nursing. A flush on his cheeks let her know that he was either uneasy or embarrassed.

"It's all right." She offered him a smile. "After what we've been through together, I don't think either of us should feel uncomfortable."

"I guess you're right." His eyes zoomed in on Amanda.

Or was he noting the fullness of Connie's breast?

Oh, for heaven's sake. There wasn't anything sexual about nursing a baby. And the fact that Connie had even let her thoughts stray in that direction was crazy.

"Look at her chow down," Greg said.

Connie gazed at her daughter, saw her tiny jaws working to draw the colostrum into her mouth.

Greg was right. Amanda had certainly gotten the hang of nursing.

"By the way," he said. "I've got Thanksgiving dinner all figured out."

"How did you do that? Did you ask Sabrina or Tori for help?" She figured he might have when he called to tell them about the baby.

"I'm sure they would have. But the roads are a mess in certain areas, so Jared and Sabrina are playing it by ear. And I just talked to Matt an hour ago. He and Tori are at the airport, but their flight has been delayed due to weather."

"What about Granny?" Connie asked. "Is she coming home?"

"No, she and Hilda are going to have dinner at the hotel this evening. But I hope they'll all be able to make it home tomorrow. And when they do, I'll have turkey and all the fixings in the oven."

"You know how to bake a turkey?" she asked, suddenly feeling even more incompetent than she had while watching her mother buzz around the set of a mock kitchen, her makeup cover-model perfect and every hair in place.

"No, I have a better idea than that. Caroline, down at the diner, is going to whip up a feast for us whenever we need it."

Connie smiled. At least he had the meal covered. And if truth be told, Caroline was going to do a much better job of it than Connie ever could have. After all, it was obvious that she hadn't been blessed with the Martha Stewart/Julia Child genes.

Or rather, the Dinah Rawlings genes.

"So," Greg said, "we'll just have our own private Thanksgiving dinner tonight."

"That sounds good. What's on the menu?"

"Mac and cheese." He grinned. "I found a box in the pantry. I hope you're okay with that."

When Joey, Sabrina's young nephew, was living here, Granny had gone out and purchased a bunch of stuff that a kid would like. There was peanut butter and jelly, too.

If truth be told, Connie wasn't a fan of processed foods, but she wouldn't admit it. The fact that Greg was trying so hard to take care of her took precedence over a dish she'd never really liked.

"I'm not big on vegetables," Greg said. "Would canned green beans be okay to go with that?"

"Sure."

She expected him to turn and walk away, yet instead he continued to lean against the doorjamb, to watch her nurse the baby.

For some reason, it seemed as though he'd earned the right, so she didn't let it bother her.

"You know," Connie said, her heart going soft and warm, "you've really gone above and beyond the call of duty for a guy who came home for a much-needed vacation."

He shrugged. "This hasn't been the start of the holiday I'd been expecting, but I'm glad I was here two nights ago. It wouldn't have been good for you to go through that alone."

He was right about that. She didn't even want to think about how much more scared she would have been.

"It's amazing," Greg said, his eyes still on the baby. "I can't believe she was inside of you two days ago. Now look at her."

Connie studied her daughter, still unable to believe she was now a mother.

The "M" word had always made her think of Dinah Rawlings, SuperHousewife.

Weird, huh?

The TV personality who knew all about creating a home out of four walls, a few appliances and a kitchen sink was actually a widow whose youngest daughter had run away from home before her eighteenth birthday. The devoted audience had no clue their daytime TV darling's life was less than perfect.

Connie glanced at the telephone on the nightstand. She wasn't about to drop the bomb yet and tell her mom about Amanda, but she should call and wish her mother and sister a happy holiday.

"Greg?" she asked. "Will you hold Mandy for me while I call my mom?" That way, if the baby woke up and cried, she wouldn't have to lie about whose baby she was.

"Sure." Greg scooped the flannel-wrapped bundle into his arms, taking the time to marvel at the sleeping newborn as he carried her out of the room.

When he was gone, Connie picked up the receiver and dialed her mother's house. Rebecca, her older sister, answered on the second ring.

"Hello?"

"Hey, Becky. It's me. I just wanted to wish you and Mom a Happy Thanksgiving."

"Oh, my God. *Connie.* Where are you? Aren't you coming home?"

"No, I'm afraid I can't this year. I have a new job, and I…need to…" Okay, so much for not wanting to lie. "I can't take any extra time off work."

"Oh, no. That's too bad. Mom and I had wanted to make this the best Thanksgiving ever, and now, without you here, it won't be."

Connie appreciated her sister's disappointment. But their mother always went to a lot of trouble, even if that meant delegating the work to others.

Everyone except Connie, that is.

No, honey, her mom used to say, *let Becky whip those potatoes. I don't want them to be lumpy.*

Here, Connie, let me do that. The flame is hot, and I don't want you to scorch the pan.

Connie cleared her throat, as though the effort might also clear the memories aside. "I can't stay on the phone long, Becky. So can I please talk to Mom?"

"Sure."

Moments later, Dinah Rawlings answered and asked the same questions Rebecca had. And so Connie provided the same answers.

"Where are you working? You're not singing with a band again, are you?"

"No, I'm working on a cattle ranch now."

"Doing *what?*"

"I'm the cook."

"You?" Her mother laughed. "I'm sorry. I can't imagine you driving a chuck wagon and cooking for a bunch of wranglers."

"Actually, I have a nice kitchen to work in."

"That's a relief. But where did you learn to cook?"

Not from you, Connie wanted to say. You were always too busy to take the time to teach me.

"I've been reading a lot of women's magazines." Connie put the rocker into motion. "So how have you been?"

"I'm great. The ratings are steadily rising. And I've been asked to make a guest appearance on Elizabeth Bronson's talk show next week."

Connie wasn't familiar with the woman or her program, but she didn't want to appear ignorant, so she offered congratulations instead.

"And how about you?" her mother asked. "You aren't still seeing…*that man,* are you?"

A year ago, Connie might have reminded her mother that the man's name was Ross. But she'd like to forget him, too. "No. I haven't seen him in a long time."

"That's good to know. You could do so much better than that."

Maybe so, but Connie had a feeling her mother would find something wrong with anyone she brought home.

"And that's exactly what I told him when he came pounding on my door looking for you," her mother added.

"Ross came *looking* for me?" Her heart rate kicked up a couple of notches. "When was that?"

"The first time was around Easter. I remember because we were going to tape a special the day he showed up. And then he came back a month or so ago. I told him that I hadn't seen you, but I don't think he believed me."

Connie's stomach clenched, and her pulse spiked even higher at the realization that Ross was still looking for her. She'd hoped that he would have moved on to someone else by now. But apparently he hadn't.

Still, Ross wasn't a subject Connie wanted to discuss with her mother. Or with anyone. He'd been her mistake. Her bad memory.

"Well, Mom…" Connie slowed the rocker to a halt. "I just wanted to wish you and Becky a happy holiday and to tell you I'm doing well."

"Where is this ranch?" her mother asked.

Did she dare tell her mother? No, now more than ever she

couldn't risk that her mother might slip up and reveal a clue as to her whereabouts to Ross.

"It's about an hour or so out of Houston," she revealed. "But I've been thinking. You live in a gated community. Why don't you remove Ross from that approved-guest list?"

"That's probably a good idea. I'll try to remember to do that tomorrow on my way to the station."

"Good." Connie blew out a silent sigh of relief. "Listen, Mom. I have something in the oven, so I don't want to go into detail now, but you were right about Ross. He *wasn't* right for me. But obviously he's not as convinced of that as I am. So if he should ever come around looking for me again, I'd rather you didn't know where I was. That way, you won't have to lie to him."

"I can keep a secret. And besides, I wouldn't risk doing anything that might provoke a reconciliation."

"Good," Connie said.

"Besides," her mother added, "I never did see what you saw in that sloppy, long-haired musician."

She winced. Greg had long hair, too. And a couple of tattoos on his arms.

Connie hadn't seen them in person, but he'd posed without a shirt on his last CD cover, his sexiest one by far.

Would her mother automatically disapprove of Greg, too?

Oh, for goodness sake. What was she thinking? The intimacy they'd shared hadn't been by choice. It wasn't…well, it wasn't real. And it certainly wouldn't lead to anything else.

To a stranger, it might appear that they had assumed Mommy and Daddy roles over the past day or so, but that was only a facade, much like the mock kitchen set that mimicked the happy home Dinah Rawlings was supposed to have created for her daughters.

"Listen," Connie said. "I really need to get back to the kitchen." Another lie, of course. Especially since Greg had assumed the kitchen duties tonight.

"I still can't get over the thought of you cooking, especially for hungry cowboys. What are you making?" Leave it to Dinah to want to know all the particulars of a menu.

"The usual holiday fare," Connie said, stretching the truth even further and making it sound a whole lot better than it was.

"I hope everything goes well this evening."

So did Connie. And, interestingly enough, she hadn't once regretted not getting to eat one of Dinah's gourmet turkey dinners. Not when she was actually looking forward to feasting on macaroni and cheese—fresh from the box—with a handsome country singer.

Chapter Four

Greg couldn't explain why he repeatedly had the urge to stop whatever he was doing and peek in on Amanda and Connie. He tried to shake off the compulsion, but it was a struggle to keep his distance, and he'd be damned if he knew why.

Maybe, since he'd never known his birth mother, he found the whole maternal/baby thing interesting.

As he was prone to do whenever he thought about being orphaned, he remembered what his aunt had told him about the night he'd been born. His mother and aunt had been traveling to Texas in a beat-up sedan, all of their belongings packed in plastic bags and cardboard boxes. It had been a long drive from the small Mexican village where the two sisters had been living, but his mother had been determined to return to the United States, where she'd been born and had grown up.

She'd taken the risk for his benefit, and had paid the price with her life.

A homebody and much shier than her younger sister, Guadalupe hadn't wanted to leave the comfort of her simple life and her home in Mexico in the first place. But Maria had been so enthusiastic, so determined and convincing, that Guadalupe had reluctantly agreed. And with her younger sister gone, Guadalupe had seen no other reason to stay in the States.

So she named Greg after the kindly priest and, after the christening, took him back to Rio San Juan, the village she'd called home. There, she raised him and loved him as her own son. Almost daily, she told him stories about his mother, a dreamer who'd had big plans for his future.

"This baby is going to be a boy," Greg's mom had told her older sister.

Guadalupe had been skeptical, of course, since Maria had a vivid imagination.

"I had a vision," Maria had insisted. "This little boy is going to grow up to become someone special someday. He might even become the president of the United States."

Greg, who'd been blessed with his mother's optimism and determination, soon came to believe it, too.

But Fate, it seemed, had a way of thwarting dreams and the best-laid plans.

Just after Greg's sixth birthday, Guadalupe, who'd never been physically strong, suffered from appendicitis. A doctor in a nearby town performed the surgery, but there were complications, and she developed pneumonia a few days later and died. With no other family to take him in, Gregorio was placed in a local orphanage. There, the boy who believed he had a destiny to fulfill became just one of a group of fifty-some children. And he'd soon found himself trying to prove both his worth and his leadership skills.

It had been a sad time in his life, he supposed. But he'd never stopped believing in himself, in the success his mother had known he would eventually find. And he never gave up believing that the United States was truly the land of milk and honey.

In the six years Greg spent living at the orphanage, he was drawn to the American volunteers who came with various church and charitable organizations and brought clothing, food and toys to the underprivileged children. They regularly made repairs to the buildings and interacted with the children, reading to them and teaching them games and songs.

Greg was brighter than most. He knew he would need to speak English if he was going to eventually move to the United States and make good on his mother's dream. So he used every opportunity to learn the language of the visitors. And by the time he was twelve, he wasn't fluent, but he'd acquired a good handle on the basics.

Time and again it had seemed that Fate had closed doors for him, but he continued to seek an open window. And then one day, while on a field trip, he had the opportunity to escape life in an orphanage and he took it.

To this day, he thanked his lucky stars that he'd eventually found Granny, that she'd been determined to be the mother he'd never known.

Of course, fitting in at the Rocking C and appreciating his new home didn't mean that he wanted to be tethered to any one place permanently. He thrived on the life he'd created for himself, on the energy he received from the bright lights and the heart-pounding intensity of the music world.

Whenever he was onstage, with his guitar in hand and the fans clapping and shouting his name, he knew he'd finally made it. That he'd achieved the life his birth mother had always wanted for him, the life he'd been destined to have.

Now, as he stood in the kitchen, fumbling with pots and pans and trying to prepare a meal he and Connie could share tonight, he had to admit it was a long way from the life he loved. But he'd be back on tour soon.

As he searched the pantry, he found the box of macaroni and cheese he'd seen earlier. He'd never been much of a cook, never needed to be. For as long as he could remember, there'd always been someone to prepare his meals—Guadalupe, the various cooks at the orphanage, Granny. And now that he was grown-up, he ate most of his meals in restaurants.

But how tough could cooking be? Besides, this particular box boasted that it was "so easy a kid could make it."

So he followed the directions and found that the claims of a quick and easy prep were true. Next he fixed ham sandwiches. After snatching a cold beer from the fridge for himself and pouring a glass of milk for Connie, he placed it all on a tray and carried it into the living room. He'd go back for the rest of that apple-spice cake afterward. Two extra large pieces was about all that was left.

As he entered the living room, he found Connie wearing a pale blue robe and standing near the fireplace. She was studying a photograph Granny had taken of Greg and his brothers on their first Christmas together.

She turned at his approach and smiled, the frame still in her hand. "This is a great picture of you boys."

Greg placed the tray on the coffee table. "That was taken about a week after I arrived at the ranch."

"It looks like you had a black eye. Did one of your brothers let you have it?"

"No. Actually, I'd been pretty battered when Granny found me hiding in her barn. That eye had been swollen shut at one time. I'd had a run-in with one of the migrant workers I'd been living with."

Connie's smile fell. "That's terrible. How old were you?"

"Thirteen."

"And you were living with migrant workers?"

Suddenly, he wasn't sure how much of his early years he wanted to share with her. Nor did he enjoy the reminder of that particular time in his life. But something in her eyes got to him, and he found the words flowing easily. "Actually, we were living and working together. But that was a very long time ago."

She glanced at the photo again. Was she focusing on how much time had passed? Or still thinking that he'd been too young for manual labor, too young to have been beat to a pulp by a man who was at least twenty years older than he'd been?

"I was born in Texas," he said, still not exactly sure why he felt compelled to explain. "But I spent the first six years of my life living with my aunt in Mexico. When she died, I was sent to an orphanage."

Connie's lips parted, and her brow furrowed in sympathy. "I'm so sorry to hear that. It must have been awful for you."

Getting sent to the orphanage? Or his escape and subsequent travels with a group of men who worked from dawn to dusk?

Both, he supposed. But it had been those first nights in the orphanage that had been the hardest. He'd cried himself to sleep more times than he could remember, and eventually, he'd gotten used to it.

Yet he'd never gotten over the struggle for identity after being thrust into a crowd of other orphans.

"Hey," he said, growing uncomfortable with the sympathy etched across her brow. "Don't feel sorry for me. It really wasn't that bad. And it made me who I am."

She seemed to think on that for a while, and he was glad to let the topic drop. But when she spoke again, he realized she hadn't let it go.

"If you were working with migrant workers when you were thirteen, you must not have remained in the orphanage too long. Were you adopted?"

"No, I ran away."

He read the question in her eyes, and while he didn't usually talk about the details of those sad, pre-Granny days, he couldn't see any real reason to keep them from Connie. Not after what they'd been through. "One day, I was in a group of older boys who were taken on a field trip to a local factory, and I wandered off by myself. I'd thought about running away many times, but I wasn't quite sure that was the route I wanted to take. But while I was on my own, I overheard two guys talking about going to Texas to work. I knew that might be my only chance to get to the States until I was finally of age, so I asked if they'd let me hitch a ride with them."

He wasn't sure if Connie would understand the burning desire he'd had to prove that his mother had been right, that he was meant to live in the United States.

"You caught a ride with strangers?"

"Looking back, I guess it was a pretty ballsy thing for a kid to do. It could have turned out badly. But I was a lot more trusting back then. I told them my father was living in Texas, and they agreed to take me to him."

"Your father lived in Texas?"

He didn't blame her for wondering about that. It was common knowledge that Granny had been a widow when she adopted him and his brothers.

"At the time, I didn't consider that a lie. I still don't, I suppose. Father Gregorio Sanchez was a priest who could vouch for my citizenship. And I was hopeful that he would tell me how to go about getting a birth certificate. He was my best hope and only ally at the time, even though I had no idea if he was still located in the same town where I was born."

"So you snuck across the border?" she asked.

"Yes. I was a U.S. citizen, but I had no documentation to back that up."

"Did the men take you to the priest?"

"No. I figured I was going to need some money. Why show up at the church flat busted and asking for a handout? So I went to work with them in the fields for a while."

"At thirteen? I thought there were child labor laws that prohibited that."

"I was tall for my age, and no one questioned it." Greg glanced at the fire in the hearth, watched the flames lick the logs. "But working in the fields wasn't all that it was cracked up to be. The labor was hard, the hours were long and there never seemed to be enough to eat."

Connie looked again at the photo from the mantel, then made her way toward him.

Greg didn't want her sympathy. Hey, he'd come out ahead. And he was stronger and wiser because of it. "It wasn't all that bad. Pedro, one of the guys I worked with, gave me an old guitar he found. And another guy taught me how to play a few chords."

A smile slid across her pretty face, lighting those green eyes in a way that made a man want to fall into their depths and never climb out. "So you got your start singing while working in the fields?"

"You could say that. I practiced every chance I got, and before long, the guys I worked with began to ask me to sing to them in the evenings."

"You make it sound easy, but I'm sure it wasn't."

"No. I'm pretty driven when I set my mind to something. But I've got a talent and an ear for music."

"How long did you work in the fields?"

"Not long. I was planning my trip to Rio Verde, where I was born, but I didn't want to show up empty-handed. So I was saving every last dime that I'd earned, and within a few months I had enough to pay for a bus ticket and still have some left over."

"How'd you end up on the Rocking C?" she asked.

"That was just a case of pure luck." Of course, he'd also wondered if being born in a church meant that he'd gotten a divine handout on occasion. "The day I was planning to leave, I went through my things, looking for the money I'd been hiding in an old can, but it wasn't there."

"Someone stole it?"

He nodded. "Yeah, but at the time, I thought this guy named

Raul was messing with me. He'd found the can one day and lifted it way over his head, playing keep-away. So I thought he might have hidden it from me."

Her brow furrowed, as though she was connecting the dots and was figuring out where his shiner had come from.

"Raul flipped out when he caught me near his bed. He accused me of stealing from him, but that wasn't true. Whoever had taken my money must have taken his, too. Raul had never been levelheaded, and he turned on me. I fought him the best I could, but he was bigger and older and stronger. He beat the crap out of me, giving me a bloody nose, a black eye and several broken ribs. He threatened to kill me the next time he laid eyes on me, and I figured that if I wanted to live to be fourteen, I'd better beat it. And the closet town was Brighton Valley."

"How'd you meet Granny?"

"Actually, I was walking down the county road, not far from the Rocking C. I was hurt and exhausted. It was nearly sunset, so I knew I'd need to find shelter for the night. I spotted the ranch in the distance and decided to hole up in the barn. The next morning, I was starving. So I knocked on the kitchen door and, using my best English, I asked the lady who answered for a job. I hoped to earn room and board until I could figure out what to do next."

"Was it Granny who answered?"

A grin stretched across Greg's face, as he remembered the day his luck had finally turned. "Yes. She fixed me a sandwich. And I wolfed it down right in front of her. She quizzed me about my parents, and while I'd planned to be evasive, she had a way of getting the truth out of me."

Connie smiled. "You don't have to tell me about that. She's pretty sick when she's pumping for information."

Greg nodded. "That's Granny for you. Anyway, she said that she had plenty of work for me. And that she'd be happy to give me room and board. So she told me to wait outside for her. I went back to the barn, where I'd left my guitar. It wasn't much, but it was all I had. One of the strings had snapped, but I'd planned to get it fixed once I earned some money."

He glanced at Connie, spotted something brewing in those pretty green eyes. Sympathy? Admiration?

Whatever it was both touched and unsettled him, yet he continued the story. "Just as I entered the barn, I heard Raul's voice. I've never been sure why he was looking for me, but I wasn't taking any chances. When he asked Granny's foreman if he'd seen me, I hid in the hayloft, afraid to let anyone know where I was. Eventually, Raul took off down the road."

"I'm surprised Granny fed you, then let you go."

"I didn't know it at the time, but she went inside to make a phone call to her friend, a retired attorney. She was tempted to call the police, but she didn't want anyone to take me away. She wanted to provide a home for me and was trying to learn her options. Little did I know that she'd recently adopted two other homeless boys and that she'd set her heart on helping me, too."

"So that's when your life took a turn for the better."

"Yes, although there were a few rough spots."

"Oh, yeah? Like what?"

"Clem, the ranch foreman at the time, tried to talk Granny out of taking me in. He reminded her that I was in the United Steates illegally, which wasn't true. I insisted that I was born in

Texas and that Father Gregorio would prove it. So Granny had Clem drive her and me to Rio Verde. And sure enough, when I introduced myself to Father Gregorio, he told Granny that I'd been born right there at the church. He showed her the birth, death and baptismal records. And then it was just a matter of time before I was cleared for adoption."

"That's quite a story," she said.

He shrugged it off. There'd been a lot of people—journalists, especially—who'd been interested in his early years, but he'd filtered the truth. His past was no one's business but his own. Not that he was ashamed of it, but life as he wanted to remember it had begun the day Granny had taken him in. And as far as he was concerned, that's all he needed to share.

Of course, telling Connie about it didn't seem to bother him. He figured that was probably due to all they'd been through together.

"So you were once known as Gregorio?" she asked.

He nodded. "Jared and Matt started calling me Greg. And before long, things fell into line. I went to school, my English improved and I made a place for myself on the ranch. Soon I was competing with them to prove who was top dog."

"I've had a chance to get to know both Jared and Matt, so I imagine you guys could get pretty competitive."

Greg smiled, thinking about the testosterone-drenched challenges that he and his brothers were always involved in. "It didn't seem to matter if it was a riding or roping contest or whether it was boasting about our baseball stats or who got better grades in school."

But there was one thing Greg was able to do that the others couldn't. He could sing and was a natural-born entertainer. Of course, his brothers always teased him about carrying his guitar with him wherever he went, but it had been the first thing he'd ever really owned. And it had become a part of him that he'd never give up.

He nodded at the picture Connie still held. "See that smile on my face?"

"Yes."

"I'd only been here a week, but Granny treated me just the same as she did my brothers. And she seemed to read me better than anyone else ever had."

"I'm not surprised. I met your mom at the clinic in Brighton Valley, and within an hour of chatting with her, she invited me home and offered me a job."

He nodded, thinking about how Granny had always seemed to know just what to say and what to do for someone who was hurting. "Do you know what she gave me that first Christmas?"

"I suppose you needed just about everything—clothes, a toothbrush…"

"She picked up all those items that very day she moved my things from the hayloft into the house. Then, on Christmas morning, when she called us all around the tree, I found that my gift was the biggest and the best of all."

"What did she get you?"

"A brand-new guitar. No one had ever gotten me a gift like that before. Something that meant more to me than anything else she could have given me."

They stood in silence for a while, and when Connie finally spoke, she said, "That's a wonderful story. You have a lot to be thankful for, too."

Yeah, he had.

Life had been tough, he supposed. Brutal even. But then he'd met Granny, and the world had opened up for him.

He loved his life now. Loved the rush, the glitz and the glamour. And now he owned dozens of guitars. Yet even though he no longer had a need for that old guitar in a musical sense, he'd kept it just the same.

It was a reminder of where he'd once been and just how far he'd come. He was on top of the world now.

And that's exactly where he meant to stay.

Connie returned the Christmas photograph of the brothers to its rightful place above the hearth, then turned to face Greg.

He was setting the plates and silverware on the coffee table, where he'd obviously planned for them to eat. She wanted to object and to remind him that it was still Thanksgiving Day, but she didn't want him to think she didn't appreciate his efforts to feed her—or anything else he'd done for her and Amanda so far.

As he emptied the tray and removed the plates, a glossy hank of his hair slid forward, obscuring his face from her view.

It was a shame, she realized, since he was the kind of man a woman could easily fawn over from dawn to dusk. Tall, broad-shouldered and with a sexy swagger in his walk, Greg was impressive, to say the least.

His olive complexion and angular features boasted the best of his Latin heritage, a heritage she shared with him.

With his coal-black hair at shoulder length and the clothes he chose to wear—frayed and faded blue jeans, along with a crisply pressed cotton shirt—Greg Clayton appeared to be both a renegade and a gentleman, contrasting traits that his fans had latched on to.

A man shouldn't be that appealing to look at, as well as so talented, Connie decided, although the women who flocked to his concerts might not agree.

"Do you want the television on or off?" he asked.

The fact that he'd considered her preference pleased her, and she hoped he wouldn't mind a truthful response. "If it's okay with you, I'd rather not have it on."

"Whatever you say." He shot her a dimpled smile that set her heart on edge and made her senses jump to attention.

Now, that's weird, she thought. She'd just given birth and should be more focused on her newborn than on a handsome bachelor, but for some reason, her hormones must be on the blink.

She turned toward the fireplace and removed two candlesticks from the mantel, then headed for the kitchen to find some matches. On a whim, she walked out on the back porch, where a single red geranium blossomed in a ceramic pot that rested near the steps.

As she returned to the living room with her hands full, Greg chuckled, those whiskey-brown eyes glimmering in a way that made her feel even more like a red-blooded woman than a brand-new mother.

"What's so funny?" she asked.

"Candles and flowers are a nice touch. But it seems a little over the top for macaroni and cheese, don't you think?"

Even the sound of his voice, which was laced with the hint of an accent, had a way of sliding over a woman like a combination of rugged denim and exotic silk.

She froze for a beat, but she quickly recovered and lobbed back a smile of her own. "No, I don't think it's over the top at all. Today is a holiday, and I want to make things special." Just the way her mom used to do when the money was tight. When everything she'd done had been out of love for her husband and kids.

"It just seems unnecessary for a casual meal," he said. "But if it makes you happy, I'm okay with it."

"My mom used to always go above and beyond for the holidays when I was a kid, so it's something I picked up from her."

"She *used* to?" he asked.

"Her career comes first now, and she doesn't have much time to go all out at home anymore. But holiday memories are important."

Connie almost added, *Especially for kids,* but Amanda wouldn't remember anything about her first Thanksgiving. And Connie couldn't explain why it was important for her to make a bigger deal out of it anyway.

It just was, that's all.

"You remind me of Granny," Greg said.

He didn't have to add that he meant that as a compliment. She knew that he did. Yet she couldn't help wondering if he found her frumpy and out of shape now. She'd always had a small waist, but when she'd taken a shower this morning and looked in the mirror, she'd wondered if the flab and the stretch marks were here to stay. Once Dr. Bramblett gave her the okay, exercise might help. And maybe some vitamin E.

As they each took a seat, she tried to focus on the food, on picking up her fork and actually digging in. Still, she couldn't help sneaking peeks at Greg, a onetime stranger who was so very far out of her league, a man who'd somehow become a...friend.

What else should she call him?

Her employer's son?

A famous country singer?

Yet just two nights ago, when he'd delivered her daughter, he'd been nothing short of a hero. And she couldn't help thinking of him that way now. Sitting down to dinner with the man felt more fantasy than real.

As a child, Connie had spent a lot of time in an imaginary world, where her only playmates were dolls and stuffed animals. Where it didn't matter that her mom and sister weren't home, that she'd been banished to her room with only a nanny to watch over her.

And it seemed that she was doing the same thing tonight. While she and Greg were merely eating together, she couldn't help pretending that they were sharing a cozy, candlelit dinner, that they...

Okay, so she might be the only one imagining that they were anything more than two people eating a nondescript meal.

Still, while she and Greg ate their dinner-from-a-box, she couldn't help thinking that they were feasting on pheasant under glass and celebrating their many blessings this evening.

If truth be told, though, she *did* have a lot to be thankful for: a healthy daughter; a warm, loving home in which to live, even if the Rocking C did get a bit hectic at times. She also had been blessed with peace of mind and refuge from the man who'd not only fathered her baby but who'd struck her one too many times and threatened to give her a lesson she'd never forget.

She blew out a slow and silent sigh.

"Do you think Granny will come home tomorrow?" she asked.

"It's hard to say. The roads should be open by morning. But knowing her, if she believes that Lester needs her, she'll stay in town longer."

"I think I'll make a couple of pumpkin pies anyway," she said. "Just in case."

"No way, Connie. I'm not going to let you overdo it. You just had a baby, and you need to take it easy. Besides, I've got food ordered from Caroline's Diner in town. There'll be plenty to eat for whoever shows up, including pie."

Connie supposed she should be happy that he was looking out for her, but she wanted to do her part. "Your mother hired me to do the cooking."

"Aw, come on, Connie. If she were here, she'd be the first one to back me up."

He was right.

Greg tossed her a crooked grin. "But I have to admit that if Caroline's Diner were open today, we'd be eating the daily special instead of this crap."

Connie would be the last person in the world to complain about the dinner he'd prepared especially after some of the crummy meals she'd fixed while employed at the Rocking C. "I'm sure this macaroni tastes a whole lot better than whatever I would have come up with."

From the first time Connie had tried her hand at cooking for Granny and the men, her failures had been legion. But Greg hadn't tasted any of those lousy meals, most of which were burnt to a crisp, rubbery or just plain inedible.

In fact, she'd quickly learned to double and triple the dessert, just so the ranch hands wouldn't go to bed hungry.

"Who do you think you're talking to?" Greg asked. "You're a *great* cook, Connie. I've tasted both your chocolate cake and that apple-spice cake."

"Cooking and baking aren't the same."

He didn't argue, and she gladly let the subject drop, as they continued to eat.

But just because she could whip up some tasty cakes and cobblers and cookies didn't mean that she knew her way around a kitchen. Not when it came to fixing meals.

Greg stiffened and tilted his head to the side, drawing Connie's interest and priming her curiosity.

"What's the matter?" she asked.

"Is that the baby I hear?"

She listened carefully, and sure enough her daughter was fussing. "I just fed her, so she shouldn't be hungry."

Connie set down her fork and began to rise, but Greg grabbed her hand and gave it a squeeze. "Relax. You stay here and eat. I'll get her."

She started to object, but something told her that he really wanted to go. That somehow, he'd bonded with the baby.

Why else would he always be asking about her, always checking on her?

The thought pleased her, although she wasn't sure why.

Before Greg reached the hallway, Amanda began to really cry out, but moments later, she grew quiet. When Greg didn't return, Connie made her way to the bedroom to peek in on them, and what she saw caused her heart to melt.

There sat Greg in the rocker, the tiny newborn cradled on his chest. The pink flannel receiving blanket had come unwrapped, and one little bootie-covered foot had slipped out. He was humming a tune she'd never heard before, and when he glanced up at her, their eyes met.

So much for wanting to pretend there wasn't anything going on between them, even if it was only one-way.

She just didn't have a clue what it could possibly be.

Or what she was going to do about it.

Chapter Five

Greg would be damned if he knew why he'd insisted upon checking the baby. He supposed it was because he wanted to give Connie time to finish eating. Or maybe because he wanted to give her a break.

Of course, it was just as likely that he found the newborn fascinating, that he actually liked being around her.

As he entered Connie's bedroom, Amanda was squirming in her bassinette and fussing. A week ago—heck, even three days ago—if someone would have told him he'd be picking up a baby without any prompting, he wouldn't have believed it. But he wouldn't have believed that he would end up being a reluctant midwife on a stormy night, either.

He carefully lifted the baby, pulled her to his chest and whispered, "Aw, *mi princesa. Que pasa?*"

Holding her close, he patted her little back the way he'd seen Connie do, yet it didn't seem to help. She continued to fuss.

"What's the matter, honey?"

A burp sounded, which must have been the problem, since she settled right down afterward. He chuckled to himself. "That was a pretty impressive belch for a princess, especially a tiny one."

Amanda rooted against him for a moment, but at least she was no longer fussing.

He reached into her bassinette, grabbed the pacifier that was lying on the mattress and slipped it into her mouth. "There you go. Now maybe you can go back to sleep."

He took a seat in the rocker, with Amanda cuddled against his chest, her knees drawn up like a little frog. As she settled in, he began to rock slowly, the antique wood creaking in protest.

The back-and-forth movement lulled him almost as much as it did the baby. Not that he was going to fall asleep, but he found the rocking motion to be calming. And right this moment, he doubted that he could have felt any warmer, any prouder, than if he'd actually fathered this little babe himself.

It was strange, though. He wasn't in any hurry to put her back to bed.

As he held her close and inhaled her baby-powder scent, he began to hum. It wasn't any particular tune, just something he'd made up on the spot. Something sweet and mellow with a rocking-chair beat.

Footsteps sounded in the hall, and he glanced up to see Connie standing in the doorway.

"I wish I had a camera," she whispered. "That would make the sweetest picture."

Greg wasn't sure he wanted that kind of snapshot to circulate in his family. His brothers would never let up on him about this. But then again, Jared and Matt had both grown softer lately, thanks to the ladies in their lives.

"A picture of you holding Amanda would be a nice addition to her baby book," Connie added.

"What's a baby book?"

"You know, it's a…" She seemed to catch herself, as though realizing that he might not actually know, that he hadn't had the same upbringing that she'd had. Then she let it go and brightened. "Well, it's like a scrapbook, I guess. Someday she'll be all grown up, and I'll have something to remind me of what she was like when she was little."

"I can't imagine her being anything other than a tiny baby."

"I know what you mean, but people say that babies grow up in the blink of an eye. She'll probably be crawling and walking before I know it."

"And then it's off to school," he said, shaking his head and studying the newborn. "I can't even imagine what she'll look like then."

"Neither can I. But I plan to cherish each moment." Connie eased closer to the rocker, then lightly ran her knuckles along the baby's hair.

Greg nodded, although he'd never given the whole kid-thing any thought. He'd never even imagined having children, nor had he thought his rough-and-tumble brothers would go that route, either. But he wasn't so sure about that anymore. He hadn't expected Jared and Matt to fall boots over heart in love, either. So who knew what might happen next?

And even though Greg, too, had softened—at least right now, with little Amanda curled up on his chest—he wasn't cut out for fatherhood. Or for serious relationships, for that matter.

Sam Marshall, his manager, was proof of that. The forty-three year old musician adored his wife, Sylvia, and their kids. But traveling with the band when they were on tour had played a big toll on their marriage, and the couple had nearly divorced a while back.

When Sylvia had told Sam she wanted out, that she was tired of sleeping alone, Sam had been heartbroken. And he'd given it all up for her.

But the music industry had always defined who he was, and Sylvia hadn't understood that.

One day, while Greg and the band were in Nashville, he called Sam and asked him to meet him for a beer. The two got to talking, and Sam told him how miserable he was. How Sylvia had admitted that even though he'd taken a 9-to-5 job, she still didn't have the happy home she'd always wanted.

Greg had suggested Sam find something else to do in the music industry, something that kept him involved, even if it was just on the fringe. Sam saw the wisdom in that, and his becoming a manager was the first step in a marital compromise and a successful alternative career. Of course, that still left him with some tension at home, due in part to the time he still had to spend on the road.

But the couple genuinely loved each other, and Greg suspected they'd finally reached a middle ground that they could both live with. Sam still traveled, but not as much. And when he was home, their family time was special. At least, that's what Sylvia had told Greg the last time he'd been at their house for dinner.

And Greg had lucked out, too. He and Sam made a great team, since Sam had one heck of a head for business.

"Do you want me to help you put the baby back in bed?" Connie asked.

Actually, he wasn't in any hurry to give her up. But he didn't dare admit it. So he said, "Sure."

As Connie reached for the precious flannel-wrapped bundle, her hand brushed against Greg's, and something warm and tingly skimmed over him. Something that seemed loaded with possibilities, yet completely out of the question.

But he shook it off as quickly as it struck. For one thing, Greg didn't date women with kids. Not that he didn't like children, but he knew better than to get involved with someone who would expect him to be at home more than a few months out of the year. After all, he was on the go more often than not, and there was no point in pretending that he would ever settle down.

Heck, look how tough Sam's traveling had been on his wife and kids. People who weren't in the business, who didn't know what it was like, just couldn't relate to that kind of lifestyle.

"That tune you were humming," Connie said. "I didn't recognize it, but I really like it. What are the words?"

"There aren't any."

"Really?" Surprise swept across her face. "You came up with that on the spot?"

"Yeah." New melodies had always come easy to him, and he'd written the music to several of his hit songs himself.

"You ought to do something with it," she said.

"Who knows? Maybe I will."

Still, it didn't seem likely. Most of the stuff he came up with usually appealed to cowboys and truckers and the honky-tonk crowd, like drinking songs and somebody-done-somebody-wrong songs.

His muse tended to shy away from lullabies and romance.

And so did he.

Still, he took one last look at the sweet little baby sleeping in the bassinette and then at the pretty mama, who stood over her with a smile that would stir the embers in a dying hearth on a cold winter night.

Again he shook off the star-crossed attraction to a woman who couldn't be any more wrong for him and tried to focus on the tune he'd just made up.

It had potential, he supposed.

As the beat and the melody played out in his mind, his muse prodded him to slip into the privacy of his bedroom and pick up his guitar, to put words to the music, even if he'd never have a reason to sing the song onstage.

Of course, it wouldn't hurt to mess around with the lullaby idea for a while, even if nothing came of it. And if it did come together for him, he could discuss it with Sam the next time they talked on the phone. His manager had a good handle on the type of songs Greg's fans had come to expect from him.

And if Sam didn't think it would fly? Then maybe Greg could let someone else record it. Someone whose fans wouldn't balk at something sweet.

Because any fool knew that lullabies and honky-tonks didn't mix.

The day after Thanksgiving dawned bright, yet the air was cool and crisp. The hands had returned to the ranch early that morning, so Greg had lined them out for the day. Then he'd returned to the kitchen for a cup of coffee, only to find Connie standing near the sink.

She was wearing a pair of loose-fitting jeans and a pale pink T-shirt. She'd also put on a bit of lipstick and mascara. She looked especially pretty today, and he wasn't exactly sure why he found her so darn appealing.

As he noted the bowls and spoons and baking supplies on the countertop, he asked, "What are you doing?"

"I'm making a couple of pumpkin pies. You can never have too many, right?" She offered him a smile, her green eyes glimmering. "And don't tell me that you don't want me baking. I feel absolutely fine. And if I get tired, I'll go lie down."

Before he could object, the engine of an approaching vehicle sounded outside. He went to the window and peered out into the drive.

"Who is it?" Connie asked.

"Hilda just brought Granny home."

Moments later, after the elderly driver had turned her car around, eighty-year-old Granny swept into the room, her cheeks flushed from the wintery air. She greeted Greg with a hug, then Connie.

"How's Lester doing?" Greg asked.

"He was doing much better last night, but I think the doctor is going to force him to retire."

"Do you have someone in mind to take over for him?"

Granny reached into the cookie jar and pulled out a raisin-and-nut-filled snack. "I was hoping Matt would step into the position. He and Tori should be here within the next hour and a half. They just landed at Bush Intercontinental and are waiting for their baggage. I'll have to talk to him about it later this afternoon." Granny scanned the room. "Where are you two hiding that baby? I can't wait to hold her."

Connie laughed. "She's sleeping, Granny. But it won't hurt one little bit for you to peek at her."

As the two women headed for the bedroom, leaving the pumpkin pie fixings on the counter, Greg couldn't help following them—at a distance, of course.

"Isn't she the sweetest little thing you ever did see?" The silver-haired woman smiled as she studied the sleeping infant.

Almost as if on cue, the baby grunted, then began to squirm.

"Well, now, look at that," Granny said with a grin. "She knows that I'm aching to get ahold of her."

Connie laughed. "I'm sure she's eager to meet you, too. Go ahead and pick her up."

Granny carefully lifted Amanda into her arms. "She's absolutely precious, Connie. Let's take her into the living room. I'd like to get her into the light so I can get a better look at her."

Greg stepped away from the doorway, making room for the female entourage to pass. They took seats on the sofa, and Granny appeared to be in her element while she cooed and marveled at the baby girl.

Granny turned to Greg, eyes growing misty. "I'm so proud of you."

"For what?" It's not as though he'd had anything to do with creating her.

"For being home when Connie needed you. For delivering the baby when no one else was here."

"Buckling under pressure hadn't been an option," Greg said. "It was no big deal."

"It was a big deal to me," Connie said, her gaze locking on his and causing everything inside of him to scamper in all directions.

"I think so, too," Granny said. "We have a lot to celebrate over dinner. So I'll have to get busy."

"Hey, you don't need to get too carried away," Greg said. "I ordered turkey and all the fixings from Caroline's Diner. All I have to do is pick it up around noon today."

"Don't forget that Matt and Tori are coming later this morning," Granny said. "And that Jared and Sabrina will be here, too."

"Are they bringing Joey and his dad?" Connie asked.

Sabrina's nephew had been staying with Sabrina while his father was in prison for a crime he hadn't committed. When the truth came out and Carlos was released from prison, Jared had offered him a job and a home on his ranch.

"No," Granny said, "Carlos is dating a woman with two little girls. I met her a couple of weekends ago and thought she was very nice. Anyway, they're having dinner together, then taking the kids on a camping trip over the weekend."

"Either way," Greg said, "I ordered enough food for an army."

His mother had never kicked the habit of picking up strays during her travels. It wasn't unusual for her to bring home unexpected guests, so she—and the cooks she'd hired over the years—had learned how to stretch a meal without making a visitor realize it. So he'd ordered extra food with that in mind.

"That's good," Granny said. "I'm glad we'll have plenty to

eat, but I still need to make my candied sweet potatoes and my butter horn rolls. It won't be Thanksgiving without them."

Several hours later, when the warm scent of baked pumpkin and nutmeg had filled the house, Greg drove into Brighton Valley to pick up the meal he'd ordered.

On his second trip from the diner to the truck, his arms loaded down with containers of food, he realized that he hadn't been pulling Granny's leg. There was definitely enough to feed an army. He must have been hungry when he placed the order.

After paying Caroline, he drove back to the ranch.

Both Jared and Matt had already arrived, and the house was hopping with activity.

The women, Sabrina, Tori and Granny, were huddled in the kitchen, fussing over Amanda. He suspected they'd each been taking turns holding her. Right now, as the others looked on, Sabrina was seated at the table, with the infant in her arms, cooing and making silly little clicking sounds with her tongue.

Uh-oh, Greg thought. His new sister-in-law was setting off some maternal vibes and wearing an I-want-one-of-these-too expressions.

He tossed a glance at Jared, his older brother, who was looking on and actually smiling at his wife. Apparently, thoughts of parenthood weren't freaking him out in the least.

Matt, who still walked with a pronounced limp following an accident that had ended his rodeo career, entered the room, and soon they were all fawning over the little newborn.

But the commotion only caused Greg to grow uneasy. They were too close to Amanda. What if someone was coming down with something?

He wanted to tell them to be careful, not to breathe on the baby. For Pete's sake, she was only a couple of days old. She hadn't had time to build up any immunity yet.

A protective streak reared its head, and he glanced at Connie, wondering if she was as concerned about germs as he was. But she didn't seem to be. She just smiled, as though she was glad the others were making a fuss over her child.

And while the baby was just as cute, just as sweet as they were all saying she was, Greg's focus wasn't on the baby right now. It was on her pretty mama.

Again, he was struck by Connie's simple beauty, something not many women had. The groupies and other performers who crossed his path tended to use makeup and clothing to their advantage. Greg had grown accustomed to appreciating a woman with spritzed-up hair, bright lipstick, tight jeans and a low-cut blouse.

But Connie was different. If anything she played down her looks. Yet there was still something about her. Something Greg found special. Appealing.

How weird was that?

Domesticity had never fascinated him before.

As far as he was concerned, fame and family didn't go hand in hand—especially if that family depended on a husband or father's daily presence to make the world go around.

Greg had always had a hole in his life, a loss that the bright lights, a thundering beat and a cheering crowd had filled.

And unlike Sam, Greg knew he would never give up what he'd found on the stage. So he'd best get his mind and his thoughts off Connie before she got the idea that he was the least bit interested in her.

He figured she'd been hurt enough in the past, and he didn't want to cause her any more pain.

Late that night, the house, while bursting at the seams with family, was finally quiet. And Greg couldn't help reflecting on the holiday they'd all spent together.

This Thanksgiving dinner had been different than the rest. Caroline's food was good, but it didn't quite compare to the spread Granny usually put out. Still, it was great being home on the Rocking C.

He'd just turned out the lights when his cell rang. At this hour, he figured it was probably a wrong number, but he sat up and grabbed the phone off the charger, which sat on the nightstand. He'd better answer, just to be sure it wasn't something important.

"Hello?" he said, trying to keep his voice down so it wouldn't wake up anyone else in the house. He glanced at the clock on the bureau. It was already after eleven.

"Greg? It's me. Hank."

Hank played keyboard in his group and was one of the best in the business. He was also a quiet-spoken man who wasn't prone to calls or chitchat.

"What's up?" Greg asked.

"Aw, man, I got bad news. *Real* bad news." Hank's voice was raw and ragged.

Greg's gut clenched as he prepared himself for the unexpected. The band had scattered for the holiday, each one heading home. But the storm had played havoc with some of their travel plans, and a couple of them had decided to drive together as far as Oklahoma City.

"What happened?"

"There was a car accident. And…" Hank choked up, and Greg could hardly breathe. "Sam wasn't wearing his seat belt again. I know we told him a hundred times, but he was…" Hank's words trailed off, as emotion stole his voice. "He's dead, Greg."

No. The breath froze inside of Greg as he struggled to make sense of Hank's words. There had to be a mistake. Sam Marshall had been more than Greg's manager; he'd been a friend.

"And…" Hank struggled to maintain control. "Patty was hurt, too."

Patty was Greg's lead backup singer. His head was spinning in both grief and shock. "How's she doing? Were her injuries serious?"

"Yeah. She's got a skull fracture, a dislocated jaw, a couple of broken ribs and a ruptured spleen. She's in surgery now."

"Where are you?" Greg asked. He had to go to his band, to his friends.

"In Norman, just outside of Oklahoma City. Are you coming?"

"Yeah, I can't catch a flight out until morning, though." Greg raked a hand through the long strands of his hair, a style Sam had told him would suit him, a style he was just getting used to. "Does Sam's wife know yet?"

Sam had been looking forward to spending the holidays at home. He'd also mentioned that he and Sylvia were looking forward to the birth of their first grandchild, a little girl who was due in February.

"Yeah. I just called her and…" Hank cleared his throat, yet

he couldn't rid himself of the emotion that made his normally deep, solid voice waver. "…Oh, God, calling her was the hardest thing I ever had to do."

Hank was just a kid himself, fresh out of high school. But he had a talent most men would give their right arm for. "Are you hurt?"

"Just a knot on my head and a sore shoulder. I was sleeping in the backseat."

"How you holding up?" Greg asked.

The kid sniffled. "I'm doin' okay. But it's tough, man. It's really tough."

"Hang in there, Hank. I'll be there as soon as I can."

"Thanks. I'll feel a lot better when you get here. The doctors and nurses keep asking me stuff like I'm the next of kin or something."

"Maybe you ought to try to get some sleep," Greg suggested.

"No, I can't leave Patty until her mama and daddy get here. The doctors said she'll probably pull through, but it's going to be a long haul."

Thank God for that.

"There's no way she'll be able to go on tour with us this winter," Hank added.

Without a manager and a lead backup singer, Greg faced the task of finding replacements or else canceling the upcoming tour, something he didn't want to do.

Something Sam wouldn't have wanted him to do.

An emptiness spread through him as the reality struck. In the past, Greg had always had Sam to take care of things, to lean on, to advise him.

And now Sam was gone.

When the line disconnected, Greg went into the kitchen. There was no way he'd be able to sleep tonight. Not now. So he put on a pot of coffee and, before it had a chance to brew, he went to the office and turned on the computer. He needed to find the first flight out of Houston tomorrow morning.

Twenty minutes later, he'd snagged a flight out of Bush Intercontinental at ten o'clock the next day. It was the first available seat that wouldn't route him through Timbuktu. With that out of the way, he poured himself a cup of coffee, then waited in the stillness of the kitchen for morning to come.

He had no idea how much time had passed when he heard footsteps padding toward him. Long enough for the coffee in his mug to cool down to room temperature, he guessed. He looked up to see Connie in the doorway, wearing a white cotton gown.

"I thought I smelled coffee," she said. Then she took a good look at his face and her expression became concerned. "Is something wrong?"

"Yeah." He scooted his chair back, thinking that he'd get a fresh cup, and stood. "Some of my band members were in a car accident in Oklahoma this evening, and my manager was killed."

Greg never cried, yet he felt his eyes fill with tears. He supposed even a tough guy like him could expect to be knocked on his butt after getting a blow like that.

"Oh, my God. I'm so sorry." Connie crossed the room in one fluid motion. When she reached his side, she lifted her arms and wrapped him in a sympathetic hug.

She didn't say anything more; she just held him.

And he held her right back.

The tough guy inside rebelled against the softness of her touch, the scent of floral soap and faint whisper of baby powder. Yet the part of him that was hurting hung on tight, absorbing every bit of comfort that she offered. As he felt a tear slide down his cheek, he held on tight, afraid to let her see how bad it hurt.

And how scared he was that the hole in his life that he'd filled had opened right back up again.

Chapter Six

Connie had only been a member of the South Forty Band for a little more than a year, but she knew the dynamics at work and understood how close a group of musicians could become. In many ways, a band was like a family, and she could only imagine the loss Greg suffered after receiving news of the accident.

As she held him close, she felt the tension in his body, the struggle not to show his emotion, and tears welled in her eyes. She wouldn't release him until he was ready to let go, until he'd absorbed all she had to give him.

Time ticked on, and she inhaled the scent of his day-old cologne—something musky, outdoorsy and male—and found herself stunned by the intimacy of their embrace. Moved by the feeling it evoked.

A dreamy part of her wondered if maybe they'd connected

on a romantic level, but she knew better than to let herself ponder something as far-fetched as that.

Greg Clayton could have his choice of women, both on the road and in every big city in which his band played.

Why would a man like him want to hook up with an unwed mother with a new baby, a woman with a rebellious and shady past?

At least, her past seemed pretty shady to her.

And while she wasn't particularly proud of her rebellious streak and some of the choices she'd made, she understood why she'd done what she'd done and how she'd ended up on the Rocking C Ranch.

Still, Connie had been fairly content with her life. At least, until Ross had started drinking more than usual and his jealous side had elbowed to the forefront. It didn't take long, and she was in trouble with him more often than not. It got to the point where he didn't want her to even give the time of day to another man.

Dang, she thought, as she held Greg close, doing her best to absorb his pain. Wouldn't Ross freak out if he could see her now.

Either way, she knew better than to let her imagination run wild. Greg Clayton was way beyond reach for someone like her.

When he slowly began to release her, she loosened her hold, too. As they faced each other again, she could see that his eyes were red and watery. That he'd been struggling with tears.

"Is there anything I can do to help?" she asked.

"I wish there was." He raked his hand through the long strands of his hair. "I'm going to have to fly to Oklahoma City in the morning."

"When will you be back?"

"I don't know. I also have to find a new manager and a backup singer before the winter tour. But I'll come home again for Matt and Tori's wedding next month, even if I can stay only a day or two."

A torrent of sadness swept through Connie like a flash flood as she realized Greg would no longer be staying at the Rocking C. That he wouldn't poke his head into her bedroom to check on her and Amanda anymore.

How weird was that? The man had all but been a complete stranger just a few days ago.

"Take good care of that baby," he said, as he struggled to regroup, to shake off his grief.

"I will."

He lifted his hand and skimmed his knuckles along her cheek. "If you need anything—anything at all—*call* me."

She tried to read into his words, into his touch. But she figured it wasn't wise to do so. He was just being brotherly, even if she could still feel the lingering warmth of his hand on her face. "I'll be okay."

"Yeah, I know." He walked toward the kitchen drawer where Granny kept pens and paper, then he scratched out his number. "But just in case, I'd feel better if you had this."

She took it and admired the solid strokes of his handwriting. "Thanks. I'll try not to bother you, though."

"Don't worry about that." His gaze locked onto hers, turning her heart topsy-turvy.

She chased away the girlish flutters that suggested there was more going on between them than there actually was. "I'm so sorry that accident happened, Greg."

"Me, too. But don't worry. I've learned how to roll with the punches."

From what he'd shared with her, she suspected that he had, but knowing that didn't make her feel any better. It made her feel sad, as she envisioned a grieving six-year-old boy being dropped off at an orphanage, the only mother he'd ever known dead and unable to keep him safe.

"Keep in touch," she said.

"I will."

They stood like that for a while, held together by some undefined thread she'd yet to recognize, then he drew back, breaking it altogether. "I'd better take a shower and pack."

She nodded, and he walked away.

Her heart went out to the handsome musician, and she realized that her own sense of loss was staggering.

She was really going to miss him.

Way more than she would have ever imagined.

Early in the morning, as the pink-tinged fingers of dawn drew back the night, Greg was packed and ready to go.

He'd talked to Hank on the telephone a few minutes ago and learned that Patty had come through the surgery okay.

Her parents still hadn't arrived at the hospital, though. Apparently, they'd gotten stranded in Chicago, thanks to the storms that had struck early in the season and had been the cause of hundreds of canceled flights over the past few days. But from what Greg had gathered while watching the Weather Channel, the skies were now clear over Houston, so he didn't expect any delays for his departure at ten o'clock.

As he entered the kitchen for a fresh cup of coffee, he ran into his brothers, both of whom had showered and were dressed for the day. He told them the news and revealed his plans to leave just as soon as he was able to say goodbye to Granny.

Both Jared and Matt were visibly sorry to hear about the accident.

"I know what you're going through," Matt said.

He did, Greg admitted. About a year ago, Matt had been involved in a fatal crash that had not only ended his rodeo career but also killed his fiancée and her young son. Matt's life had been pretty bleak at that time, but then he'd met Tori and fell in love.

Now Matt was busier than he'd ever been, keeping the books on the Rocking C, flying to Wyoming to purchase broodmares for an equine partnership he and Granny had established and overseeing the construction of his and Tori's new house. With a Christmas wedding planned, Matt's life had taken an exciting new turn.

To be honest, Greg didn't think he'd ever seen him as happy as he'd been lately—even before the accident, when he'd been making a name for himself on the circuit.

Jared left his coffee mug on the table, where he'd been sitting, and stood. "Is there anything we can do, Greg?"

"No, but thanks for asking." Greg put his hand on Matt's shoulder and gave it a squeeze. "But come hell or high water, I'll be back for your wedding, even if I can't stick around very long."

"Good." Matt had insisted on having both of his brothers stand up with him, claiming he had two best men. The Clayton boys might compete at just about everything, but there was one thing they didn't argue about—their love and respect for each other.

Jared extended a hand to Greg, his grip firm. "Take care, little brother."

"I will."

Greg crossed the room and opened the pantry door to get a heat-resistant paper cup he could take with him. Just as he snagged one, Granny entered the room. He greeted her solemnly then announced that he was leaving and explained why.

"Oh, honey." His mother crossed the room and wrapped him in her arms. "I'm so sorry to hear that."

He accepted her gardenia-scented love and support, then pulled away and cleared his throat. "I know you are, Granny. And thanks."

"I'll have my church pray for all of you—Sylvia, Patty and the rest of the band."

Greg never had been very religious, but he appreciated his mother's faith and her prayers. "Thanks." He nodded toward the door. "I'm going to get my bag, then head out of here. I'll give you guys a call after I get settled."

"Please do," his mother said.

He poured himself the coffee he'd come for and ambled toward the doorway that led to the rest of the house. There was one last goodbye he wanted to make, even though he and Connie had pretty much taken care of that a couple of hours ago.

For a man who'd traveled all over the country on tour with his band, he had his choice of women. So this bond or whatever he felt for Connie didn't make a whole lot of sense. But he'd had this incredible…well, an urge to protect both her and the baby, he guessed.

At first, he'd suspected that it might have something to do with curiosity and with his never knowing his biological mother, a woman who would have surely loved him like Connie loved Amanda.

But there was more to it than that.

Last summer, when he'd first met her at Granny's eightieth birthday party, she'd turned his head. And he hadn't even known she was pregnant then.

Greg had no more than stepped one foot down the hall toward Connie's bedroom when he heard her humming a familiar tune.

His tune, the lullaby he'd been working on—or rather, messing around with. Of course, he hadn't quite gotten it right yet.

But she had. She'd added some words to the tune and had put her own spin on it. And as he continued to listen, to slide into the beat and absorb the words, he couldn't help thinking that her rendition was better than his.

Caught up in the melody that was more than a simple lullaby, he stood still for a while, struck by the crisp, clear quality of her voice.

And riveted by it.

Maybe his song had needed to be sung by a mother, by someone who could actually reflect the right emotions.

Finally, when Greg realized that he needed to be at the airport by eight o'clock and that he'd better get moving, he continued on to Connie's room. She looked up when he entered, ending the song immediately.

"That was great," he said. "I like what you did to it."

"Thanks."

For some reason, he couldn't let it go at that. She had one of those voices that seemed to linger long after a song was done, and he couldn't believe that she didn't know it, that no one had recognized it yet. "Have you ever sung professionally?"

His words, it seemed, hung in the silence, and as his gaze locked on hers, he awaited her response.

It was an easy question, Connie realized. One that only required a yes or no, but even though her lips parted, she paused for the longest time, struggling with the answer.

Was Greg thinking about having her audition for his band?

Surely not. But if he was, she was flattered—to say the least. Yet there was no way she had the kind of talent required to sing backup for someone of Greg's caliber.

"No," she said. "Not really."

He cocked his head. "What do you mean, 'Not really'?"

She wasn't sure how much she wanted to tell him.

"Did you ever perform for an audience or sing for money?" he asked.

"Yes," she admitted. "And I got paid for it—although not very much. But certainly not to sellout crowds or in Las Vegas."

Singers like Greg couldn't possibly relate to the kind of gigs they'd had. The South Forty Band had performed only at seedy bars and hole-in-the-wall joints.

"I'm really not what you'd call a professional singer," she threw in for good measure.

And even if she had been, it wouldn't matter now. She had a child to take care of. A baby girl who needed her mommy at home.

"How long did you perform?"

Was this some kind of interview? If so, he was barking up the wrong tree.

"I sang with a band about a year or so, and to be honest, there were times when I liked what I was doing. But I was young and naïve back then. And it's a time in my life that I'd like to forget."

Yet talking about it released the memories she'd tried to lock away.

She'd only been eighteen when she'd left home for good and had been forced to work at jobs that didn't require any particular skills. At night, she would hang out at a local bar, where she used a fake ID whenever she was carded.

A year later, she took up with Ross Flanders, a bass player in a wannabe country-western band. Against her mother's pleas and threats, she moved in with him—something she now regretted.

Ross was the first to notice that she had merits and talents of her own—her singing voice for one—and he soon suggested that she perform with his band in some of the honky-tonks and bars in town.

She'd told him no time and again, but he'd pleaded and prodded until she'd finally given in. He'd been right when he'd told her that standing on a stage was a thrill in and of itself. But there'd been a cost, too.

"I'm going to be auditioning to find someone to take Patty's place in the next week or so," Greg said. "Why don't you come and sing for me."

Even on a good day, Connie didn't have the voice or the training to be the kind of singer he needed. "I'm not what you're looking for."

"Let me be the judge of that."

"Sorry," she said. "I'm not interested."

He shrugged. "Suit yourself."

"Good luck with the search, though. I hope you find a replacement soon."

"Thanks. I won't settle for just anyone. I'll cancel the winter tour first."

She knew he had to be fussy about the person he chose, although she didn't think he would actually cancel, that he would let down his fans. The magazine articles she'd read about him had all commented about his dedication. Once, when he'd been at the Grand Ole Opry in Nashville, he'd performed with a 102 temperature rather than cancel or postpone the show.

He watched her for a moment, which made her wonder if he still had some lame idea about her filling in for Patty.

"Do you miss it?" he asked. "The stage, the singing, the applause?"

"No, I don't." She didn't miss the band she'd been a part of, or the gigs they'd had. And she certainly didn't regret having a life without Ross. "Besides, I'm not cut out to sing in front of an audience."

"You never know."

Oh, yes, she did. And even if she was fool enough to believe that she could tour with one of the top bands in the country, even if she didn't have any qualms about dragging a baby from city to city and raising her backstage, there was one more thing that affected her decision.

There was no way she'd want Ross to catch wind of where she was.

Nine months might have passed since that last time they'd been together, but the cuts and bruises were still too fresh in her memory, his threat still too real.

He hadn't always been a jerk, but the more he drank, the worse he got. His first act of violence had been a shove that knocked her to the ground. She'd hurt her ankle that day and had hobbled around for a week.

The second time, he twisted her arm until she feared he'd broken it. He hadn't, though. The doctor at the emergency room had said it was just a sprain.

The next time, when he'd hit her with his fist and split her lip, he'd cried after he realized what he'd done. He swore up and down that he'd learned his lesson, that he'd stop drinking and would never risk hitting her again.

He'd been so sorry that she'd forgiven him.

But he just couldn't stay away from the booze.

The guys in the band had tried to encourage Ross to enter rehab, pointing out that his personality changed whenever he drank, but he refused to even consider it, saying he wasn't the one with the problem. As a result, the guys blamed Ross for the band's inability to rise above low-paying gigs and gave him the boot.

They'd begged Connie to stay, though. And she'd agreed.

Ross was beside himself with anger and jealousy. And guess who reaped the bulk of his wrath?

When he still refused to seek help, Connie had ended things between them. Or so she'd thought. Ross started following her around. Stalking her.

The last time she'd sung with the band, they'd been playing at a rinky-dink bar in the middle of nowhere, and a young, drunken cowboy who was barely twenty-one had come up to her during their break. He'd told her that he loved her, that he wanted to take her home to meet his mama.

There wasn't a person within hearing distance who would have thought the guy meant anything by it. He was not only smashed, but he was also harmless.

But Ross had flipped, accusing her of messing around on him. Out in the parking lot, his rants had escalated, and when she tried to go back inside, he struck her repeatedly with his fist. The police were called, and Connie pressed charges.

That night, as they were hauling Ross away, he told her she was going to pay for turning him in. And that once he got out of jail, he was going to drag her back home—where she belonged.

Believing he would make good on his threat, Connie cut her waist-length dark hair and had it highlighted. Then she packed her bags. For a while, she'd pondered running home to her mother, but she was afraid she wouldn't be welcomed with open arms. Dinah's show had finally become syndicated, at least through the Bible Belt, and many of her viewers were conservative.

Her mom was, too. She'd never liked Ross because he was in a band and had long hair, and she'd never understood why Connie had moved in with him, and in retrospect, Connie wasn't really sure, either. She supposed it had been one more way to rebel, to embarrass her mother.

For that reason, going home with her tail between her legs wasn't a pleasant option.

Then, just when Connie thought that things couldn't get any worse, she learned she was pregnant.

So rather than face her mother's shame or live in fear that Ross would eventually follow through on his threat, she decided to create a new life for herself and her baby in a place where she'd be safe.

And she'd found all that and more at the Rocking C with Granny.

Now Greg was hinting that she should consider giving it all up. That she get up on a stage again, this time in a bigger arena. But even if, for a tiny second, she could imagine herself there, she couldn't risk having Ross find her.

"No," she told Greg again. "I'd never consider being a part of a band again."

"Why not?"

Needless to say, she had a lot of reasons for not wanting to perform again, but she chose to share only the most important one. She glanced at the sweet newborn in her arms, then back at Greg. "Why should I chase fame when I'm holding all the treasure I need?"

Greg reached for Amanda's hand, reverently lifting it as he studied each tiny finger while she continued to sleep. "She's something special, that's for sure."

A miracle, Connie thought. A blessing she'd been gifted with on a dark and stormy night.

She looked to Greg, who'd released the baby's hand. "I've already told you this, but I don't know what I would have done without you when I went in labor."

Their gazes locked, and she lost herself in those whiskey-brown eyes. Whatever kept swirling around them flared again, and this time, it was so real, so warm, so vibrant, that she could almost grab ahold of it. And, if she had managed to grasp it, she might never have let it go.

"I'm glad you weren't alone that night," he said. Then he looked at the alarm clock on the bureau. "I'd better get out of here. I've got a plane to catch."

Words and thoughts clamored in Connie's throat to get out, but all she dared say was, "Take care."

"I will." Then he cupped her jaw with his hand and brushed his thumb across her cheek.

A flurry of warmth and emotion tumbled in her chest, and she wondered if he felt it, too.

Probably not. Once again she feared she was reading something into his friendship, his kindness.

"Kiss Amanda goodbye for me," he said.

She nodded, not trusting herself to speak. As he withdrew his hand from her cheek, the heat of his touch lingered on her skin. Her eyes watered, and she blinked back the tears that threatened to spill.

While he turned away, an aura of sadness seemed to hover over him, causing his shoulders to slump a bit. Yet in spite of the tragic news he'd just heard and the grief he now carried, he walked through the open bedroom door with strength and determination.

As soon as he was out of sight, as his footsteps grew dim, Connie's own sadness was almost overwhelming. And she'd be darned if she knew what to do to make it go away.

She missed Greg already—more than she dared to admit. And while she suspected that his grief, his loss, had become her own, a growing ache in her heart suggested it might be more than that.

But there was nothing she could do about it.

Other than wait for his return and hope that his smile would make things right again.

Chapter Seven

The week before Christmas, the wedding preparations were in full swing, and a sense of anticipation filled the air. It seemed that everyone had a multitude of jobs to do, both on and off the ranch.

Matt was working from dawn until dusk each day, supervising the hands, overseeing his new horse-breeding venture and keeping the books. He was also staying on top of the contractor who was building the new house he and Tori would live in, a split-level home that sat on a knoll near the creek.

Tori, who'd gotten a job working with Dr. Bramblett in Brighton Valley at the clinic, was also taking care of the many last-minute details of the wedding that was to be held at Granny's church on Saturday.

Connie had done everything she could to help, so she'd been

busy, but that didn't mean she hadn't found time to think about Greg. She wondered how his hunt for a new manager was going and whether he'd found a backup singer to temporarily replace Patty.

He'd called several times since he'd left, insisting that he'd be home for the wedding. But he'd yet to return, and Connie found herself missing him more than ever.

Whenever she heard a vehicle in the drive, she would peer out the window, expecting to see that he'd finally arrived. But each time her hopes had soared, only to be dashed.

He'd been gone for nearly four weeks now. Was he thinking about Amanda? Would he be surprised to see how much she'd grown?

Connie glanced at her daughter, who was sitting in her swing in the kitchen, lulled by the automatic motion and the music. Then she returned her attention to the big pot of chicken and dumplings she'd fixed for tonight's dinner.

After living with Granny for more than eight months, Connie had finally begun to feel competent when it came to creating a dinner menu and preparing meals that were more than just edible.

Her mother probably wouldn't agree, but then Connie no longer tried to win her mom's praise.

Or her affection.

As Granny entered the house through the mudroom, Connie replaced the lid on the pot that had been simmering on the stove, looked up and smiled. "Dinner will be ready soon."

"Good, I'm hungry. And I suspect Matt and Tori will be, too."

"I'm sure they will be. They've been working hard, especially with the new house and the wedding plans."

Now that Tori was working at the clinic in Brighton Valley and was no longer cleaning the ranch house, Connie tried to pitch in as much as she could. But with the baby and the cooking, she wasn't able to get to everything. So Granny had hired a woman to come in once or twice a week to do the big chores.

"Did you know they plan to move into that house before they leave for their honeymoon?" Granny asked. "I imagine the cabin they've been staying in is pretty cramped."

Tori hadn't complained. And quite frankly, Connie thought it made the perfect little love nest. "I'm sure they're just eager to start their lives together."

"You're probably right."

"By the way," Connie told Granny, "that dumpling recipe you gave me was really easy."

"It's also tasty." Granny made her way to the sink, washed her hands and dried them on a paper towel. Then she stopped by the stove and, after lifting the lid, peeked inside the pot. "Mmm. It smells delicious. You've sure come a long way, Connie."

"I have you to thank for that, Granny. I can't believe you gave me a chance, especially when I didn't have any experience. And then you hung in there with me, even when I kept messing up."

"How else were you going to learn?"

She had that right. As badly as Connie had wanted to cook, she'd never had the chance.

Nine months ago, when Connie first met Granny, she'd just moved to Brighton Valley and her savings account had taken a beating. She'd needed a job badly, but other than singing and baking, she didn't have any real skills to offer an employer. So her worries about being able to support herself and the baby had been mounting.

Then, while seated in the waiting room at the clinic in Brighton Valley, Connie met Granny. The elderly woman had been friendly, but she'd also been inquisitive. Connie had tried to answer her questions honestly, but she'd wanted to protect her identity and her privacy.

However, when Connie stood to go to the restroom, she fainted and collapsed on the floor. Granny was soon at her side and, before long, had offered Connie a job that paid a decent salary and provided room and board.

Needless to say, in no time at all, Connie had shared her life secrets with the kindhearted woman.

Of course, there'd been a downside to the job offer, since Connie had never learned how to cook. And the position on the Rocking C required her to make hearty meals for a bunch of hungry wranglers. But Granny hadn't been the least bit concerned about that.

"If you're going to be a mother," the older woman had said, "then you'll need to learn how to cook. And I intend to give you that opportunity."

It would have been nice if Connie's mother had taught her those skills, as she'd done for Becky. But she hadn't. Instead, she'd claimed that it was easier for her to do things herself or to hire it done. And since she had always been pressed for time, Connie had felt as out of place as a prom-night pimple on a teen girl's chin.

But it hadn't always been that way. When Connie's dad had

been alive, she'd been the little princess—at least for the first ten years of her life. And everything had been fairy-tale perfect.

In the eyes of an adult looking back, Connie suspected it might not have been a perfect life for her parents, though.

Ricardo Montoya had been a struggling Latino businessman when he'd met and married an Anglo wife. But he was also a dreamer with big plans for success.

Unfortunately, and in spite of all the hard work he put into his business venture, it never quite took off.

Still he and Dinah were blessed with two daughters, and as far as Connie knew, their marriage was relatively happy.

Dinah had been a homebody back then, a loving woman who thrived on being the perfect mother and making a happy home for her husband to come home to.

But then Ricardo was killed in a freak industrial accident, leaving Dinah to support two daughters and to pay off a slew of creditors. Her only marketable skill had been an innate ability to make a house into a home—and often on a shoestring budget. So on a whim, she offered to give tips to homemakers during the end of a local television news show that aired in the mornings.

The host decided to give her a try, and when the ratings rose, she was given her own show. Before long, Dinah had become the talk of the town and the queen of the coffee klatch crowd. But her success was bittersweet, at least as far as Connie was concerned. Because while Dinah practically flaunted her homemaking skills on television, she no longer had time to make her own house a home. Instead, she'd hired a maid, a nanny and a cook.

"Your mom would be proud of you," Granny said, as she washed her hands in the kitchen sink.

Connie had her doubts.

At one time, she'd wanted nothing more than to gain her mother's respect—and her affection. But not anymore. She'd learned to live with the fact that Becky had an active role in the show. And that Connie's only contribution had been to dress appropriately and smile during the holiday specials, something she'd grown tired of doing as a teenager.

Of course, competing with her sister or her mother didn't matter anymore.

"I know that your mother was working hard to support you kids," Granny added. "So I'm sure she didn't have time to teach you how to cook. But she certainly could have asked her housekeeper to offer some advice or guidance."

That was true, but Connie had been chased out of the kitchen more times than not. So, in an attempt to find a place in her mother's life—or more specifically, on the show—Connie went to a local cooking school. It might have proved to be an embarrassment for her mom, but since the two went by different names, no one ever knew that Dinah Rawling's youngest daughter didn't know her way around a kitchen.

Of course, the only class that fit in Connie's high school schedule at the time was Delectable Desserts.

She'd learned to make sweets and goodies that rocked, and when she decided to pick up a part-time job, she landed one in a bakery, where she could hone her baking skills.

Unfortunately, the job didn't last. When the shop owner, a kindly old woman in her sixties, decided to retire, Connie found herself unemployed.

And lonelier than ever.

"I'll be so glad when the wedding day is here," Granny said.

"I'm sure you will." Connie knew that Granny had been secretly hoping that her sons would settle down and get married. And she'd seen the oldest two fall in love this year—first Jared last March, then Matt a couple of months later. "Weddings are a happy time. Is their house finished yet?"

"Just about. There are a few odds and ends that need to be done yet, but they're going to start moving in tomorrow." Granny took in a deep breath, then sighed. "I'll be happy when the wedding is over so they can take off on their honeymoon. I just hope he isn't too pooped to…" Granny smiled. "Well, you know what I mean."

Connie laughed. "I suspect he won't be too tired for *that.*"

"Well, either way, I'm eighty years old now, so if I'm going to get to enjoy my grandchildren, the boys will have to get busy."

"At least you have Amanda to hold and spoil until then."

"I'm thrilled about that. And for the record, I want you to know that I consider her my first grandbaby."

Connie smiled and gave Granny a hug. The woman had a heart as big as Texas, and being taken under her wing had been Connie's biggest blessing.

"You know," Granny said, "you're welcome to live with me as long as you like. But once Tori moves into the new house, the cabin will be empty. So it's yours if you want it."

Connie had been so happy to have her own bedroom at the Rocking C that she hadn't even considered having a home of her own. But if truth be told, she'd love to have a little more room. "Thanks, Granny. I think I'd really like that."

Maybe then Connie could re-create the feeling of hearth and

home that her mother's television career stole from the Montoya family. Or, at least, what it stole from Connie.

A vehicle drove up, and Connie realized it was probably Matt, who'd been out at the new house. He'd be hungry, no doubt. "I'll have dinner on the table in about five minutes."

"All right." Granny strode to the window and peeked out. "Well, I'll be darned. Look who's finally home."

Greg?

Connie's heart somersaulted in her chest.

If her assumption was true, it was the best news she'd had in four long weeks.

It was nearly dinnertime when Greg turned into the driveway and headed for the ranch house. As he slowed in front of the barn, he was met by the cattle dogs, both of which were barking up a storm.

"Hey, settle down," he told the Queensland Heelers as he opened the car door. "Don't you recognize me? I'm not a stranger."

Yet, as he slid out of the driver's seat, he had to admit that he really hadn't spent much time at home in the past few years.

As the dogs began wagging their tails and nuzzling against him, he realized they hadn't completely forgotten him or his scent after all.

He greeted them each with scratches behind their ears and a few well-placed pats. Then he grabbed his travel bag and his guitar from the backseat.

It was good to be back, he thought.

Earl Clancey, one of the ranch hands who'd worked on the

Rocking C for years, had been walking out of the barn when Greg arrived. He lit up when he spotted Greg and approached the car. "Well, look what the cat drug in."

"Hey." With a canvas carry-on bag in one hand and his guitar in the other, Greg acknowledged the man with a grin and a nod. "How's it going?"

"All right." The lanky, fifty-something cowboy slapped a hand on Greg's back. "It's good to have you back, son."

"Thanks. It's nice to be home again."

The cowboy peered into the backseat and, apparently spotting a few of the gifts Greg had brought with him, asked, "You need any help with this stuff?"

"Actually, if you don't mind, I've got some presents in the trunk, too. So I could use an extra pair of hands." Greg shuffled the bag so that he could give Earl the keys. "Just give me a minute to put this stuff in the house, and I'll be right back."

"Sure enough." The lanky cowboy studied the remote door lock he held as though he'd never seen one before, but he figured it out on his own and popped the latch on the trunk.

Greg was nearly to the house when he heard Earl let out a long, slow whistle. Obviously, he'd found it jam-packed with gifts.

"Boy, howdy," the cowboy called out. "You weren't kidding. What are you gonna do? Play Santy Claus?"

Greg was usually pretty generous at Christmas, and for a moment, he wondered if he'd overdone it. But what good was it if a man couldn't share the fruits of his labor with his friends and family, especially when he rarely came home these days?

Besides, the family was growing, and he'd added more people

to his shopping list this year. Still, rather than offer an explanation or an excuse, he climbed the back steps and entered the house through the mudroom.

Granny was in the kitchen, facing the rear corner, her back to the door he was entering. Yet as much as Greg loved and missed his mother, it was Connie he was looking for. And his search was quickly rewarded.

She stood with her back to the counter, and when she turned, their gazes met, she tossed him a grin. She was wearing a pair of light blue jeans and a cream-colored blouse, nothing the least bit noteworthy or sexy. Yet she looked good.

Damn good.

And it made him glad to be home.

"Hey," he said.

Her smile illuminated the room and set his pulse soaring. "You're back."

"You say that like you didn't think I would be."

Granny, who'd apparently been seeing about the baby, turned to face him, a broad grin softening the wrinkles on her face. She was holding Amanda, who'd gotten a heck of a lot bigger since Greg had last seen her.

He set his bag on the floor and his guitar on the table. Then he eased closer to Granny, closer to the baby. "Wow. Look how big she's gotten in the past few weeks."

"She's outgrown her newborn outfits," Connie said.

"Well, in that case, I'm going to have to give her one of her Christmas presents early." Greg caressed the baby's head, felt the softness of her wispy dark hair. "She even looks different. More like a real baby, I guess."

The mudroom door swung open, and Greg turned to see Earl coming into the house, his arms loaded down with gifts.

"I'd better help him." Greg turned and headed outdoors.

When he returned with an armload himself, Granny asked, "What did you do? Buy out all the stores?"

"Just about." Greg chuckled. "I have two new sisters-in-law to shop for this year, as well as Joey and Carlos. And I also picked up a wedding gift for Matt and Tori." He didn't mention that he'd picked up stuff for Connie and the baby, too.

"Can I get you to carry those presents into the living room?" Granny asked Earl. "They need to go under the tree. That way, Connie can set the table."

Greg snatched the pink package away from the others. "This one doesn't go under the tree."

"What's that?" Connie asked. "A present for Matt and Tori?"

"Nope. This one is for the baby."

When he handed the pretty box to Connie, she took it and studied it carefully. Then she drew it to her chest and held it close. "Maybe we should wait until Christmas."

"Don't worry, Amanda will have plenty of presents. So go ahead and open it now."

"But…"

"It's a birthday gift. That's why it's wrapped in pink paper." Greg wanted to see the look on Connie's face when she saw what he'd found. In fact, when he purchased the gift, he'd been thinking about her, about her response.

She carefully removed the girly, polka-dot bow. Then she tore at the paper, trying to be careful not to completely destroy it.

When she lifted the top of the box and drew back the tissue, she gasped in delight. "Oh, Greg. How cute is this?"

He watched as she pulled out the little Western outfit he'd purchased, the dinky pair of baby-soft denim jeans, the white eyelet top and tiny pink socks that looked like cowboy boots. Then she looked at him, surprise and pleasure splashed across her face. "It's adorable. I love it."

Something had told him that she would. "It's supposed to fit a three-month-old baby, so it'll be way too big for her now."

"That doesn't matter. I can't wait to try it on her, even if she swims in it." She flashed him another appreciative, bright-eyed grin, and he was glad that he'd asked the sales clerk to wrap it up, which had made the surprise so much more effective.

Boot steps sounded from the living room, as Earl returned for another handful of gifts.

Granny, who'd been tagging along behind him, crossed the room and handed the baby to Greg. "Here, honey. She's been missing you."

"You think so?" he asked, taking the sweet bundle and trying not to make goofy noises and faces when he held her. But the truth was, he'd missed her.

He'd missed her mama, too, but he wasn't ready to admit that. And he probably never would be.

Granny, her hands now empty, picked up some of the packages and carried them back to the living room, leaving Greg and Connie alone in the kitchen.

"How's the search going?" Connie asked. "Did you find a new manager?"

"It's been tough trying to find someone to replace Sam, but

I lucked out a couple of days ago. Gerald Grainger has been in the business for years, and I think he'll do a good job."

"And the singer?" Connie asked. "Did you find someone to go on the winter tour with you?"

"Not yet." Greg was looking for a certain style and sound, but he hadn't found it yet. "Gerald is going to hold another audition tomorrow. If he finds someone, he'll let me know. But I'll have the final say."

"I'm sure the right one will come along."

So was Greg, but he couldn't help wishing that Connie would agree to audition and wondering if she would measure up. She might not be the right person to replace Patty, but he suspected she might come close to what he was looking for, what he needed.

And he wasn't just talking professionally.

Connie seemed to measure up to every woman he'd ever known in a lot of ways. There was a beauty about her that had nothing to do with the clothes she wore or the makeup she used.

Maybe that's what he found so appealing—her simplicity.

There'd never been a shortage of women trying to win Greg's attention, if not his heart. But none of them had struck his fancy in a permanent way before.

Yet he had to admit, Connie was coming pretty darn close.

The weather could always be a bit unpredictable in December, but Saturday, the twenty-first of December, had dawned bright and clear. It was a lovely day for a wedding.

Earl had driven the women to town and had dropped them off earlier at the church.

Connie had been eager to see the quaint building again in the daylight. Last night, when they'd arrived for the rehearsal, she'd been charmed by the interior.

Yet in the light of day, she'd been even more impressed with the structure as a whole.

Built in the 1880s, Brighton Valley Community Church had been in constant use as a place of worship ever since. With its white clapboard walls, stained-glass windows and a classic steeple, it was a charming place for a wedding. And Connie was convinced that Tori and Matt would have a wonderful memory of their special day.

Their first job had been to set out the wedding cake that Connie had baked and decorated. It was square, with each of the four layers alternating flavors—white and chocolate. It had a mocha and fresh strawberry filling, which Tori had requested. And the buttercream frosting had been adorned with real flowers.

Even if Connie did say so herself, it had turned out every bit as lovely as the picture in the bridal magazine. And she suspected the guests would be just as pleased with the taste.

After Connie was convinced that the cake was displayed the way it should be, the church wedding coordinator directed the women to the choir room so they could get dressed.

Now it was nearly one o'clock, according to the clock on the wall. Just moments ago, the wedding coordinator had come in to say that the wooden pews were packed with family and friends waiting to wish Matt and Tori their best.

Connie watched as Sabrina carefully tucked the veil securely into Tori's red hair, which had been swept up in a feminine mass of curls. Her winter-white gown, a Victorian style with tons of lace and tiny seed pearls, fit right into the historical setting, as did the dusty-pink dresses Connie and Sabrina wore.

"I'm nervous," Tori said.

"Don't be." Connie placed a kiss on her cheek. "I've never seen a prettier bride."

"Thank you." Tori wrapped one arm around Connie and the other around Sabrina. "I'm so glad you both agreed to stand up with me."

Tori had a younger sister, but it had been the women she'd met at the Rocking C whom she'd chosen as bridesmaids.

As the music began, the door swung open, and the coordinator returned. "It's time."

As the women filed out to begin the processional, Connie clutched a bouquet of pink roses. When the coordinator nodded, she started down the aisle.

For a moment, it was easy to imagine herself as a bride, and she wondered if she would ever experience a candlelit, flower-filled day, if she would ever wear white lace and make romantic promises to the man she loved.

She smiled as she walked slowly, her eyes on the three brothers who were waiting in front of the altar. They were dressed in formal Western wear—black boots, slacks, jackets and hats. Crisp white shirts and bolo ties rounded out their outfits.

Matt, who'd spent months in a wheelchair earlier this year, was proudly standing without the use of his cane.

When Jared's eyes lit up, Connie realized Sabrina had started her walk and that the bride would soon be next.

Yet it was Greg's gaze she sought, Greg's smile.

When she reached the front row, she slid a glance at Granny, who sat next to her friend Hilda. The two elderly women had volunteered to look after Amanda, who was sleeping peacefully through the ceremony.

As Connie took her place at the altar and Sabrina soon followed, the organist struck the chords that announced the beginning of the "Wedding March."

Tori's grandmother sat across the aisle from Granny, holding a dainty handkerchief and dabbing at her eyes. She was seated next to Tori's younger brother and sister. From what Connie had gathered, there had been a rift of some kind between the siblings, but they'd patched things up a few months ago.

As Tori started down the aisle, the wedding guests stood, and several of the ladies pulled out tissues from their handbags. But it was the watery glimmer in Matt's eyes that touched Connie and turned her heart to mush. What she wouldn't give to have a man be that much in love with her, that happy to claim her hand in holy matrimony.

Again, Connie looked at Greg, and their gazes locked. Yet she didn't dare imagine him being the man she might someday marry. It was too big of a stretch.

"Dearly beloved," the silver-haired minister began, drawing Connie's attention to the reason she was here.

As the ceremony continued, she clutched her bouquet and stared straight ahead.

Tori and Matt had written their own vows, and Connie couldn't help but blink back tears at their touching professions of love. But that hadn't been the only surprise for the wedding guests.

The bride and groom had no more than finished their heartfelt promises when Greg reached behind the altar, where he'd apparently hidden his guitar. Then he introduced a song he'd written for Matt and Tori. As he began to play, and Connie looked out into the pews, she realized that the romantic love song had clearly stirred the hearts and souls of everyone who'd gathered in the church.

But no one had been more touched, more moved than Connie. Maybe because she knew all it needed was a feminine voice as a backup.

She knew that Greg had written quite a few of his own hits and suspected that this one would be his biggest yet.

After the minister proclaimed the couple husband and wife, Matt and Tori strode back down the aisle arm in arm, followed by Jared and Sabrina.

Greg reached out to Connie, and she took his arm. He escorted her out of the church and to the fellowship hall, where the reception would be held.

"That was absolutely beautiful," she whispered.

"The wedding?" he asked.

"Well, yes, it was. But I was talking about the song."

"Thanks." He guided her into the hall that had been decorated with cream-colored roses and Christmas greenery.

"Are you planning to record it?" she asked.

"I don't know." He walked her toward the punch bowl, and for some reason, neither of them commented about the fact that she still held his arm when it was no longer necessary. "It's not my usual style."

"Maybe not, but I still think you should consider it."

"Why?"

Her fingers, which gripped his muscled forearm, picked up the beat of his pulse, and she felt even more connected to him. More bound.

"Because the words brought tears to just about everyone's eye," she said. "Because it has one of those melodies that sticks with a person for a long, long time. And because I know your fans will love it, especially the women. I think it's destined to be a standard wedding song for years to come."

"If you're that convinced, then maybe I ought to try it out during my winter tour and see how the fans react."

She knew exactly how they'd respond. And a part of her wished that she could be there to hear the applause, the enthusiastic reception. But there was no chance of that.

Greg poured them each a glass of punch before downing his in short order. Then he escorted her to the reception line, where they were to greet the incoming guests. Connie took a sip of her drink, then stashed it behind a floral arrangement so she could fulfill her obligation.

When they'd finished the formalities and the photographer had gotten all of the shots that he'd wanted, Greg and Connie went their own ways.

She'd had to field an array of compliments on the cake she'd baked, and she'd thanked everyone. But she was eager to check on Amanda.

As she approached Granny, who was holding the baby now and enjoying all the added attention the child drew, she asked, "How's she doing?"

"She's been an angel," Granny said, "but she's getting a little fussy. I think she might be hungry."

"You're probably right." Connie retrieved her daughter and took her into the choir room to feed her. If the gown she was wearing had been styled differently, she might have been able to feed the baby discreetly in the fellowship hall, but as it was, she thought it was best to slip away.

Yet Greg's song continued to play in her mind, and she soon found herself humming it to Amanda.

When the baby was finished and had been burped, Connie changed her diapers. "There you go, sweetie. Now let's go back to the party."

Moments later, as she and Amanda entered the fellowship hall, Sabrina spotted them in the doorway and approached. "There you are. I was looking for you."

"The baby was hungry." Connie glanced down at her gown. "And I had to practically undress to feed her."

Sabrina smiled and placed a hand on Connie's shoulder. "I don't envy you for that, but if you ever get tired of holding her, I'd be more than happy to take her off your hands."

Connie was warmed by the thought of how many people had accepted her and her daughter. "You know, she's going to really be spoiled if I'm not careful. There's always someone wanting a turn to hold her. But I think it's important for a child to be loved. My father once said that everyone deserves to be the apple of someone's eye."

As Sabrina reached out her hands, Connie passed her the baby.

"She's the sweetest thing," Sabrina said. "I can't wait to have one of my own."

"Are you and Jared trying to get pregnant?" Connie asked.

"Well, let's just say we're not doing anything to prevent it."

Granny would be pleased to hear that.

As Sabrina cuddled Amanda and whispered to her, Connie entered the fellowship hall, looking for the glass of punch she'd set aside earlier. She found it right where she'd left it.

The band, she decided, wasn't anything to shout about, but it didn't seem to matter. The guests appeared to be pleased, and the bride and groom were too busy looking in each other's eyes to be aware of anything else.

"Hey," Greg's voice sounded, drawing her full attention, as well as a smile. "Dance with me. You're way too pretty to be a wallflower."

The glimmer in his eye told her he meant it, so she thanked him. And when he reached out a hand, she took it.

It had been ages since she'd danced, and while the band ended one song and began another, she and Greg waited for the beat.

"You're beautiful, Connie. And dressed in that fancy gown, you look like a princess."

"Thank you."

Holding his hand, seeing the blatant appreciation in his eyes, she felt like a princess, too.

And that had to be quite a change.

He'd seen her at her worst. Her thoughts immediately drifted to this morning, when he'd seen her wearing an oversize shirt that had been adorned with a splatter of spit-up.

Maybe she ought to put a little more effort into her dress, into her makeup.

As soon as the thought formed, she squelched it. What was she thinking? She knew better than to make a play for Greg Clayton.

He might be gorgeous and the kind of crush-sparking man any grown woman still breathing would fawn over, but he wasn't someone a single mom like her should pin her heart on.

And even if he was as willing to take their friendship to a romantic level, Amanda deserved to have so much more than a daddy who came in and out of their lives like someone pushing through a revolving door.

And so did Connie.

The music started again, but instead of a Texas two-step beat she'd been expecting, the band played a slow song. That didn't seem to faze Greg, though. He drew her into his arms, and she followed his lead.

But as he held her close, as they swayed to the beat of a romantic ballad, she closed her eyes and savored the musky scent of his cologne. For this moment, she was Cinderella and he was her prince.

But they weren't royalty. And they weren't characters in a fairy tale. They were just friends.

But as Greg pulled her closer and their hearts beat as one, Connie wasn't so sure about any of that.

Chapter Eight

The wedding celebration ended at four-thirty in the afternoon, when Matt and Tori took off for Bush Intercontinental Airport and a honeymoon trip to Costa Rica.

Granny wanted to stay at the reception until the last guest went home, so Greg and Connie had plenty of time to secure the baby's car seat in his rental SUV. When the older woman finally joined them in the parking lot, Connie offered to let her sit in front, but Granny wouldn't hear of it. "I'd much rather ride in back with the baby."

So they all piled into the car, and Greg drove them to the ranch.

About a mile down the road, Connie glanced over her shoulder at Granny. "I'm afraid I got so caught up in the wedding excitement that I haven't given dinner much thought yet."

"Don't worry about cooking anything," Granny said. "Matt

told the hands to have dinner on him at Caroline's tonight, so it'll just be the three of us. And to be honest, I'm not at all hungry. I ate two helpings of that wedding cake you baked. I can't believe how beautiful it was. Or how tasty. You've certainly got a gift when it comes to whipping up sweets and desserts."

"Thanks, Granny."

Greg slid a glance across the console at Connie, his smile reaching somewhere deep inside of her. "You really outdid yourself today, Connie. That cake was out of this world."

Of all the compliments she'd received so far, Greg's meant the most. "Thank you."

"Where did you come up with that idea?" he asked.

"Tori had found a picture in one of the bridal magazines, and I tried to re-create it. I'm glad it worked."

"You know," Granny said, "since Tori and Matt officially moved into their new house yesterday, the cabin is empty now. So anytime you're ready to set up housekeeping is fine with me."

Before Granny had actually pointed out "the cabin" to her, Connie had envisioned the place as a log structure. However, it was really a small, wood-sided house that sat on a block foundation and boasted a front porch, where a couple of potted plants flanked the door.

In March, it had been a home to Sabrina and after that, to Tori.

While Connie was eager to move in and create a home for her and Amanda, she didn't want Granny to think she was in a hurry to leave the house. And she had to admit, she also liked having Greg nearby, where he was able to poke his head into the room every now and then to check on Amanda.

Of course, after dancing with him at the wedding, after

feeling his arms wrapped around her and the rush of romantic yearnings his embrace had evoked, things might be different.

And if she stayed too close to him for much longer, she might set herself up for disappointment or heartbreak.

"I certainly appreciate the offer," she told Granny. "It will be nice to have a place of my own."

"I thought you might want more privacy," Granny said, "now that you have the baby."

Uh-oh. Had Amanda been making more noise than Connie had realized? She nibbled on her lip, wondering if Granny was hoping to get some peace and quiet.

"Moving into the cabin won't be a chore," Connie said. "I really don't have much stuff to take with me. Just a few personal items, my clothes and the crib."

"Don't forget the little dresser I gave you for Amanda's things. You'll need to take that with you, too."

Was it Connie's imagination? Or was Granny encouraging her to move out—and quickly?

"I suppose I could move in tonight," she said. "As long as someone will help me with the bigger items."

"Greg will help. Won't you, son?"

He glanced across the seat at Connie, his gaze intense, his expression unreadable. "Sure, I'd be glad to. But don't you want to wait until morning? It'll be dark soon."

"Whatever's easiest," Connie told him. "But it might be nice if you two got a good night's sleep tonight. And since I have very little stuff to take with me…"

"The baby's cries don't bother me at all." Greg glanced into the rearview mirror.

Connie wasn't sure if he was looking at the baby who slept in her car seat or sending a silent message to his mother.

Apparently, the baby hadn't disturbed him, but she had serious doubts Granny would ever admit she'd been bothered. Yet she hated to put out her kindhearted employer any more than she already had.

"Actually," Connie said, "I'm really looking forward to having a place of my own. So, if you wouldn't mind helping me, I'd appreciate it."

Thirty minutes later, while Greg was getting the crib and dresser from the ranch house, Connie stood inside the bedroom in the cabin. On the center of the queen-size bed, Amanda dozed in the infant carrier that detached from the car seat.

As Connie surveyed the room, she realized that the bed was adorned with a new goose down comforter and shams that matched the white eyelet curtains. She wondered why Tori had left it behind.

It didn't matter, she supposed. It just struck her as odd, that's all.

As she began to unpack her suitcase and to place her personal items—makeup, toothbrush and paste, shampoo and conditioner—into the bathroom, she realized Tori had left cleaning products under the sink. And toothpaste and shampoo in the medicine cabinet.

She'd also cleaned the place, which was incredibly nice, considering how busy she'd been this past week.

After putting away the last of her things, Connie proceeded to the kitchen to see what Tori had left and what she'd taken with her.

In the pantry, she found coffee, some canned goods, peanut

butter, spices… There was a bread box on the countertop that had a loaf of whole wheat and a package of bagels.

In the fridge, she saw milk, orange juice, eggs, and condiments.

Why had Tori left all of this food behind? Why hadn't she taken it to her new place?

As Connie closed the refrigerator door and turned toward the dinette table, she spotted a note resting under a potted plant.

> Dear Connie,
> Something tells me you will be the next one to move into the cabin, so I left as much behind as I could. Granny insisted upon purchasing new bedding and some groceries. She also hired a cleaning lady as a surprise. I hope that you find as much happiness within these four walls as I did.
> Take care. I'll see you when we get home.
> Tori

What a sweetheart Granny was.

Then Connie's movement slowed as the wheels began to turn.

When she'd arrived at the ranch last March, the weathered and neglected cabin had been empty for nearly ten years. Sabrina, the first to move in, had cleaned it from top to bottom and had given it a fresh coat of paint—inside and out. She'd only begun the refurbishment when she fell in love with Jared, got married, and moved north to live with him.

So then Tori had picked up where Sabrina had left off, adding a few loving touches of her own.

But both women had moved into the cabin before falling in love with one of Granny's sons.

A lovely coincidence? Or part of some maternal game plan?

Was the privacy Granny had insisted Connie needed just a ploy and part of some kind of romantic setup?

"Oh, Granny," Connie whispered. "You might want to see all three of your sons married and with families of their own, but this is one match that isn't going to work."

Connie hoped that the good-hearted woman would realize that a success rate of two out of three wasn't bad.

She returned to the small living room and studied her new abode. In spite of Granny's far-fetched hopes, Connie would enjoy settling in and putting her own mark on the cabin.

She scanned the dark paneled walls, the stone fireplace and rough-hewn mantel. Her new home might be a far cry from the sprawling four-bedroom house in which she'd lived during her high-school years, but it would soon hold more warmth and love.

A television with rabbit ears rested on a makeshift table that had been created out of boards and a couple of cinder blocks, yet it seemed to fit right in with the ugly furniture—a black Naugahyde sofa, a green vinyl recliner, a retro-style floor lamp—all of which made the house appear rustic.

But the new curtains Tori had made both brightened and softened the worn, secondhand decor.

Connie turned back to the fireplace, where a mason jar on the mantel held a couple of artificial hydrangeas.

Next December, if she was still living here, she would decorate the room with greenery. She would also hang a stocking for Amanda. But since there were only four more days until

Christmas Eve, meals to cook for the hands and holiday baking yet to do, her time was stretched to the limit. So all that would have to wait.

Heavy footsteps sounded on the porch, as someone strode across the wooden plank flooring. Connie went to the door, expecting to see Greg. Yet her breath caught when she spotted him on the porch, holding the frame of the disassembled crib.

He appeared so daddylike, which didn't at all seem to fit with his image as a famous country singer.

She quickly opened the door and watched him carry the crib frame to the bedroom and lean it next to the window.

He glanced at the sleeping baby, and a slow smile stretched across his face. *"Que preciosa."*

Amanda *was* precious, and it warmed her heart to hear Greg say it in Spanish. It made his words seem so...heartfelt, so genuine.

Just the sound of a male voice uttering such a sweet phrase in her father's native tongue brought back loving memories of the man who would have adored Amanda, in spite of the circumstances surrounding her conception.

Connie followed Greg back to the living room.

Instead of heading for the door, he stopped and turned. "I almost forgot. Granny wanted me to tell you that there was a message for you from your mother on the answering machine. She must have called while we were at the wedding."

"Thanks."

"You know," Greg said, scanning the small but cozy room. "I'm going to pick up a Christmas tree for you tomorrow. They're selling them in that empty lot next door to the feed store in town."

"You don't have to do that."

"I know, but I want to." He reached out and cupped her jaw. His gaze locked onto hers, and his thumb caressed her cheek, sending her pulse topsy-turvy. "Something tells me that Christmas won't be the same for you without one."

Had she been that easy to read?

He slowly removed his hand and let it drop to his side. "I'll be back with the mattress."

"Thanks, Greg. I appreciate your doing this for me."

"You're welcome." For a moment, something buzzed and sparked between them, but she'd be darned if she knew exactly what it was. At least, on his part.

He nodded toward the telephone on the lamp table. "Don't forget to call your mom."

"I won't."

Connie knew what her mother wanted, what she expected. And she was going to have to tell her no.

As Greg headed back to the ranch house, leaving Connie alone, she decided that she had put off talking to her mother as long as she dared. So she picked up the receiver and dialed her mom's cell.

Her mother answered on the third ring. "Dinah Rawlings."

Still so efficient, so professional.

"Mom, it's Connie."

"Oh, honey! Where are you?"

Connie realized that Dinah wasn't really asking where she was; she was actually more concerned about where she *wasn't*. And that was at home.

"I'm at a ranch outside of Houston, remember?"

"Well, yes. Of course. But we're taping the special tomorrow. You're coming, aren't you?"

"I have to work," Connie said, even though she knew Granny would let her have the time off if she asked.

"But it's the Christmas show, honey. You know how important this is."

Did she ever. *In the Kitchen with Dinah* and all the holiday specials had been a priority in her mom's life for almost as long as Connie could remember.

Dinah clicked her tongue. "The viewers have come to expect seeing our family together, honey. They send cards and letters afterward, telling me how nice it is to see how you girls have grown up over the years."

Yeah, well, they'd really flip if they ever learned that Connie had "shacked up" with a man—one who'd grown violent and who had fathered her illegitimate baby.

"You know that I'd be there if I could," Connie lied. "But I'm afraid it's just not possible this year."

"Could you at least write a Christmas message to Becky and me? Something I could read over the air?"

"Sure," Connie said, compromising in the only way she could. "I'll come up with something and e-mail it to you tomorrow morning."

"Thanks, honey." Her mother fumbled the phone, then must have turned on a faucet.

"I hear water running," Connie said. "What are you doing?"

"Trying to talk to you and get ready at the same time. I have a speaking engagement for one of the local churches this evening, and it's being televised."

So what else was new?

An ache settled in Connie's heart, forcing out what little hope she'd harbored for a better mother/daughter relationship. Apparently, her nearly yearlong absence hadn't had much of an effect on her mother's priorities.

She listened as her mom attempted to apply makeup or dig through the closet or something. And she wasn't sure if she should feel slighted or honored that her call had been taken.

Snagging an excuse to end the conversation and to ease the pang of disappointment, Connie said, "Well, I know how busy you are. So I'd better let you go."

"All right. I really do need to get ready," Dinah said. "But while you're on the line, I want to ask you something. Did you ever call Ron?"

Gosh, her mother never had been able to get his name right.

"You know," Dinah went on to say, "the long-haired guitar player you were dating? The last time we talked, I told you that he stopped by looking for you."

Connie again rolled her eyes. "His name is *Ross*. And no, I haven't talked to him and don't intend to. He wasn't a very nice person."

"I could have told you *that*," her mom said.

Maybe so, but Connie wouldn't have listened back then. After years of playing second fiddle to everyone and everything in her mom's life, she'd gotten tired of it all and had spent her teenage years rebelling by dating boys her mother wouldn't have approved of—if her mom had actually come home long enough to meet any of them.

Eventually, the housekeeper had snitched on her, which had resulted in a major blowup.

Connie had even run away from home once, only to be

dragged back by her mother. "What are you doing?" Dinah had asked once they'd gotten into the privacy of the car. "Are you trying to humiliate me?"

Her response had been a shrug, but deep inside she knew that causing her mother embarrassment had been a contributing factor, at least on a subconscious level.

But those days of rebellion had passed.

"Are you dating anyone now?" her mom asked.

Had she asked out of maternal interest or professional concern?

Connie couldn't be sure, but opted for honesty. "No, I'm not seeing anyone."

"That's probably for the best."

Was it? The heat of anger bubbled to the surface, but rather than lash out, as she'd been prone to do when she was younger, she tamped it down the best she could. "Okay, Mom. I made a mistake getting involved with Ross, but I've dealt with it. So I'd appreciate it if you wouldn't bring it up again. And for the record, if I ever decide to date again, it won't be anyone's business but my own. I'll decide who and when—and I'll deal with the consequences, good or bad."

"I'm sorry," Dinah said. "I didn't mean to make it sound like I told you so, but…"

But she had, and they both knew it.

The sound of something breakable hitting something solid clanked in the background.

"Oops," Dinah said. "I just knocked my pancake makeup into the sink."

"Listen, Mom, I know you don't have time to chat right now. So I'll let you go and talk to you later."

When the call ended, Connie hung up. Yet the past and the painful memories kept the connection alive.

For as long as she could remember, she'd wanted to create a home of her own, a life that she had some control over. And in a sense, she'd managed to do that.

Yet as footsteps again sounded on the porch, and Greg entered the house carrying the crib-size mattress, she realized there were some things in her life that she hadn't planned on.

Like Greg Clayton being a part of it.

Greg woke up late the next morning, and by the time he got to the kitchen, Connie had the food on the table—a hearty breakfast of hotcakes, scrambled eggs and bacon. He greeted her and the baby, but since the hands were seated around the table, he didn't take time to chat.

After he'd eaten his fill, he went into the office to check his e-mails and to use the telephone. He needed to talk to his new manager about a couple of issues he had regarding the upcoming tour, which, with any luck, would get underway in early January.

And one of those issues included the hunt for a backup singer. Assuming they could find someone before New Year's Day, they'd only have a week or so to practice with her. So he dialed Gerald Grainger's number and waited for an answer.

A deep voice tinged with a Southern twang sounded over the line. "Hello?"

"Gerald, it's me, Greg. How are things going?"

"Everything's on track. I've got the travel arrangements all made, although I'll still need to secure a couple of airline tickets for the singer. But I can't very well do that until we know who it'll be."

"How did that audition go yesterday?"

"Not bad. We had about twenty try out so far. For the most part, they all did fairly well, but no one really stood out. I did hear one that I'm going to ask to come back for a second audition. Her name is Callie Sue Dennison, and she has a great voice. She's a looker, too, so I think she'll work out. 'Course, I'm not sure if you'll agree."

"Why is that?"

"You said you wanted someone who sang like a honky-tonk angel, and while I think I know what you mean, I'm really not sure this gal is what you're looking for. You're going to have to listen for yourself."

"Set something up with her for the day after Christmas," Greg said. "I'll fly out and listen to her."

"Will do," Gerald said. "I sure hope you like what you hear. Otherwise, it's going to be tough getting someone else ready before that tour starts."

Yeah, Greg realized that. "For what it's worth, I've been checking out a woman who lives in this area. And I'd really like to have her come to that audition after Christmas."

"Oh, yeah? You want me to set something up with her?"

"No, I'd better take care of that. I'm still working on her. At this point, she's not interested in going on the road."

"Even with Greg Clayton and his band?" Gerald's tone held a sting of surprise. "You've gotta be kidding me. If I held an open audition, I'd have hundreds of singers lined up for that position. What's the deal?"

"I'm not sure. But for one thing, she just had a baby."

"Some people drag their kids along on tours. So if she sings as good as you think she does, we can work through that. Although, to be honest with you, I'm not really looking forward to tripping over a bunch of rug rats."

That wasn't surprising. Gerald had never been married and didn't have children, which was one reason Greg had hired him. There wouldn't be a family to pressure him while he was on the road.

"Don't worry," Greg said. "The woman I'm talking about doesn't really have kids. She's only got one little baby."

"Then that won't be tough. We'll just hire a nanny to go on the road with us."

That's what Greg was thinking. "If she can bring the baby along and knows that we've got someone qualified to look after her while we're practicing or performing, it just might work. But she hadn't been interested when I talked to her before."

"Maybe she's just jockeying for more money," Gerald said.

"I don't think that's it."

"Then what's the problem?"

"Just the baby, I think." Greg leaned back in his seat, and the springs creaked. "Now, keep in mind that I've only heard her sing a couple of lines. But she seemed to have what I've been looking for. And she's had some experience. So I'll keep working on her."

"Well, if anyone can charm a woman, it's you."

Maybe Greg had done so in the past, but Connie was different. She didn't have stars in her eyes, and she wasn't the kind of person who was tempted by fame or impressed by bling. At least, she didn't seem to be.

"Talk to Callie Sue," Greg told his new manager. "And give me a call when you've got things set up."

When the line disconnected, Greg returned to the kitchen to talk to Connie about the audition, only to find that she'd already cleaned up the mess from breakfast and had taken Amanda back to the cabin for her morning nap.

It was a bit chilly today, so he didn't like the idea of her taking the baby out, even if she did bundle her up.

What was she going to do when it rained?

That was why he hadn't been keen on her moving out of the ranch house so soon.

Okay, to be honest, that wasn't the only reason. A part of him wanted to keep her and the baby close. But he couldn't very well admit that, not without giving her and his mother the wrong idea. After all, Granny had made no secret that she'd wanted to see all of her sons married. And he didn't want her to start playing matchmaker, like she'd apparently done with Jared and Matt.

So he'd agreed to help Connie move, especially when she'd told him how important it was to her.

It hadn't been a chore at all. Other than the crib and dresser, there hadn't been anything else for her to take. It was obvious to him that she hadn't come to the Rocking C with much more than a few clothes.

Most of the women Greg knew didn't even know how to pack that light.

He glanced at his watch and saw that it was already after nine. Maybe now was a good time to drive into town and purchase that tree he'd promised to get her. He'd love to see the look on her face when he set it up in the cabin. Of course, he'd have to pick up some decorations while he was at it. He'd also ask Granny if she had any ornaments to spare. It was the least he could do for her while he was still here.

After Christmas, he'd be on his way—with or without her.

So he drove into Brighton Valley and picked out a small, four-foot noble fir. It wasn't anything fancy, but it would do.

After he'd delivered the tree and set it up in the cabin for her, he would ask her again to audition.

Who knew? Maybe this time she'd agree. But if not, he'd keep working on her.

If he was going to have a new woman travel with the band, it might as well be Connie.

He couldn't think of anyone else he'd rather have with him, although he refused to ponder why.

While Amanda napped, Connie used the time to get some of her Christmas baking done. To be honest, even though the kitchen in the ranch house was a whole lot roomier and had a much bigger selection of supplies, she preferred to work in the cabin.

Funny how it had begun to feel like home so soon.

When the timer went off, she pulled out a batch of sugar cookies from the oven. Then she removed them from the pan to let them cool. The little Santas, bells and stars came out perfectly, and she looked forward to frosting them and adding colored sprinkles.

Footsteps sounded on the front porch, followed by a rap at the door. So she set the spatula on the counter and went to see who it was.

Her breath caught when she found Greg wearing a heart-strumming smile. He held the trunk of a small Christmas tree in one hand and a plastic shopping bag in the other.

The light wintry breeze had blown a strand of hair across his face and splashed a tinge of color on his cheeks.

There was something precious about his boyish expression, and she felt compelled to wrap her arms around him and thank him properly. But she forced herself to hold back.

"You got a tree," she said, standing aside so he could enter.

"I told you I would."

Yes, but he'd been spending a lot of time on the phone recently, trying to stay on top of that winter tour, and she hadn't really expected him to follow through.

"Where should I put it?" he asked.

She placed an index finger on her bottom lip, then scanned the room and pointed to the far corner. "Over there, I suppose."

"If it were earlier in the month, I would have gotten you one of those stands that holds water, but with Christmas Eve only two days away, I figured it wouldn't be up long enough to need it." He set the four-foot tree where she'd instructed, then took the plastic sack he'd been holding and set it on the recliner. "I also picked up some lights and ornaments to put on it."

"You have no idea how much I appreciate this. Amanda won't remember this Christmas, but I will."

He dug through the plastic shopping bag and withdrew two strands of colored lights. Next he pulled out a small box and handed it to her.

"What's this?" As she turned it around, she saw that it held a pretty pearl-colored bulb with a couple of handpainted teddy bears on it. Across the front it said: Baby's First Christmas.

The gift, his thoughtfulness, touched something deep inside of her, and emotion balled up in her throat. As she blinked back tears, she responded the only way she knew how and gave him a hug. But as he wrapped her in his arms, enveloping her in warmth and strength, she forgot what she was thanking him for.

Instead, she closed her eyes and relished the feel of his embrace, the musky scent of his cologne. His hand slid along her back in a caress that seemed sensual…yet so natural.

A heady rush of pheromones swirled around her, and she was lost in something more than appreciation, more than a hug between friends. As she felt the vibrant and steady beat of his heart, she realized she was in trouble.

Big trouble.

She was falling head over heels for Greg Clayton, in spite of her resolve to keep things light.

That wasn't a good idea. She was setting herself up for disappointment, especially since he would be leaving on tour in the next week or so and returning to the bright lights of the stage and the high-profile life he'd created for himself.

As she slowly drew back, ending their embrace, she tried to shrug off the growing sexual attraction, the yearning for more than friendship.

"I can't wait to decorate the tree," she said, "so thank you for getting it for me."

"No problem."

"If there's anything I can ever do for you…"

A slow grin stretched across his face, and those whiskey-brown eyes glimmered. "As a matter of fact, there is."

Had he smelled the goodies she'd just baked? Maybe picked up the scent of sugar and vanilla?

Thinking that he might appreciate some milk and cookies, she smiled. "What is it?"

"I want you and Amanda to fly with me to Nashville the day after Christmas. And then I'd like you to audition."

She stiffened. "I told you I wasn't interested in singing professionally."

"I know. But it would only be for the winter tour. You could quit after that. And we can take Amanda with us. I'll hire a nanny to look out for her while you're singing. She won't feel the least bit neglected."

Connie's stomach clenched as she thought of all the other reasons she didn't want to ever be onstage again.

"It's just for a couple of months," he pressed. "It wouldn't have to be permanent."

She knew he was in a bind, and if there was any way to help him out, she'd do it. But she couldn't agree to go on stage without risking the sense of safety she'd found at the Rocking C. So she said, "I can't do that."

"Why not?"

She supposed she could give him a couple of reasons, but then she'd have to tell him that she'd screwed up. That she'd let flattery go to her head. That she'd been so intent upon rebelling that she'd hooked up with a guy who'd been terribly wrong for her.

And even if Greg understood and didn't make her feel foolish about her mistakes, there was always the possibility that her mom's viewers would find out.

At one time, that wouldn't have bothered Connie in the least, but she'd outgrown the need to punish her mother for putting fame ahead of family.

No, her reasons were many and complicated, so she chose not to explain them at all.

"I just can't."

"Will you at least think about it?"

She didn't have to because the biggest reason hung over her head like an ominous storm cloud.

What if Amanda's father found out where she was and made good on his threat? What if he learned that they'd created a child during their time together? What if he made Amanda's life miserable, just as he'd once made hers?

No matter how badly she wanted to help Greg out of his bind, no matter how much he'd done for her and Amanda, she couldn't agree.

Because each time she thought about revealing her face publicly, Ross's parting words rang in her ears.

You're going to pay for this, Connie. And you'll think twice before you cross me again.

Chapter Nine

Just after lunch, while Greg was in the office, Connie knocked lightly on the door.

"Am I interrupting anything?" she asked.

"No, not really." He looked up from the computer screen. "What's up?"

"Earl's at the front door. He wants to talk to you."

"Did he say what he wanted?"

"No, but he looked a bit perplexed."

Before Matt took off on his honeymoon Saturday evening, he'd left the crusty old cowboy in charge of the ranch. So Greg figured something may have come up that he wasn't able to handle.

As Greg made his way to the front door, Earl removed his dusty hat and ran a hand through his thinning hair. "Blasted teenage drivers."

"What happened?" Greg asked.

"A little redheaded girl who'd only had her license for a couple of days was driving too fast along the county road about an hour ago. And when a coyote ran out in front of her, she swerved to avoid it. She missed the damn critter but took out about twenty-five yards of our fence along the north pasture."

"Oh, no," Connie said. "Was she hurt?"

"Nope." Earl blew out a ragged sigh. "But she broke her fingernail and took on like it was the end of the world. She called her daddy, and he came by to look at the damage. Said he had insurance. But we can't wait to replace that fence. A couple of cows got out already."

"How bad is it?" Greg asked.

"It's not going to be a simple fix. Why don't you come take a look? I hate spending a man's money without an okay."

"All right." Greg reached for the hat he'd hung at the door, then followed Earl to the corral, where they chose a horse for Greg to ride.

Just getting back in the saddle again felt good. So did getting sweaty and dirty. For the first time in ages, Greg enjoyed a real workout and the chance to be one with the land.

It also helped keep his mind off his troubles, as well as Connie.

When he'd taken that tree to her this morning, she'd thanked him with a hug, but he'd had a hell of a time letting go of her. She felt so warm, so soft, that he'd wanted to run his hands all over her, to take that embrace in a different direction altogether.

There'd been a hundred different reasons why he didn't need to lose his head over her, but he'd be damned if he'd been able to think of a single one of them at the moment. So he'd held her longer than he should have before heading back to the house.

Still, he hadn't been able to shake thoughts of her or that peach scent for the rest of the morning. And he'd had a difficult time keeping his eyes focused on his plate during lunch.

He'd showered before dinner. Yet even as the day wore on, thoughts of Connie had dogged him.

After a dinner of spaghetti, salad and garlic bread, he'd gone into the office and made a few calls, one of which was to Patty. She'd been released from the hospital a couple of weeks ago, but her recovery was going to be long and rough.

"I'm sorry about leaving you and the band in such a lurch," she said, her voice altered by a wired jaw.

"Don't worry about that," he told her. "I just want you to get better."

They talked a bit about Sam, who'd died in the accident, and how difficult his death had been on his wife and kids. But Greg didn't mention how tough Sam's loss had been on him. He hadn't needed to; everyone in the band knew the two had been close.

After ending the call, Greg thought about going into the family room and clicking on the television, but he decided to walk over to the cabin instead. He'd gotten used to checking on Amanda before he turned in at night. At least, he'd been using the baby as his excuse. He actually liked talking to Connie, too. Especially when the house was quiet and they were alone.

He wasn't sure what the mother and baby were doing to him, but he found himself more and more determined to figure out a way to take them on the road with him and the band—whether Connie wanted to sing or not.

As he hiked along the darkened path that led to the cabin, the light from the barn, as well as a three-quarter moon, allowed him to make his way without mishap.

The curtains were closed, but a soft yellow glow from the lamp in the living room suggested that she was still awake. As he reached the front porch, he could hear singing from within.

The voice, earthy yet angelic, rang out strong and clear. "…Round yon virgin, mother and child…"

Damn, he thought. Her voice had a Patsy Cline style of its own—soulful, heartbreaking. The kind that echoed in your mind long after the last chord was played.

He eased closer, making sure he stayed clear of the wooden porch. Connie might have refused to audition for him, but at least he had a chance to hear her now.

When she'd finished the last chorus of "Silent Night," he still didn't make his presence known. Instead, he went back to the ranch house for his guitar, then returned to the cabin and knocked.

"Who is it?" she asked from behind the closed door.

"It's Greg."

She answered wearing a white cotton gown, a pale blue robe and a smile. "Hey, this is a nice surprise." Yet she fingered her lapel as though she was nervous. He wasn't sure why she would be.

Of course, she tended to unbalance him some, too.

She stepped aside, allowing him into the cozy living room, with a fire burning in the hearth. The place suited her, he decided.

What had she done to make it seem so...homelike? Maybe it was the tree, which she'd adorned with the lights and ornaments he'd brought her.

"I thought I'd come by and see Amanda," he said. "If that's okay."

"It's fine. But why'd you bring your guitar?"

"I've been messing around with that new song I wrote and wanted your opinion on something." He looked around the small living room. "Where's the baby? Is she asleep? I don't want to wake her up."

"It's okay. She likes music." Connie pointed to the infant carrier that sat a few feet away from the Christmas tree. "I just fed her and let her watch the lights until she fell asleep. I was going to carry her to bed when you came."

He strode closer to the seat, where the baby dozed peacefully.

"I'm getting ready to pour myself a glass of milk and eat a cookie," Connie said. "Do you want to join me?"

Greg smiled. "Sure. It sounds like a Christmasy thing to do."

Connie walked to the kitchen, and he watched her go. Moments later, she came back with a tray that held a small platter of decorated sugar cookies and two glasses of milk, which she placed on the coffee table.

Greg took a seat on the sofa, and Connie sat next to him— close enough for him to get a whiff of her peach scent.

He wasn't sure what would taste better, her or those cookies.

Dang. Even his sweet tooth was opting for Connie.

"So what did you do to the song?" she asked. "I liked the way you sang it at the wedding."

"I figured it would work better as a duet, so I created a female part." He hadn't actually done that, but it was the best ploy he could come up with. "Faith Hill and Tim McGraw have done some fabulous songs together. And I think this one ought to be performed in the same way."

Her brow furrowed as she gave his idea some thought.

He reached for his guitar and began strumming the chords, just as he'd done at the wedding. Then he sang the romantic words he'd written for Matt and Tori. When he finished, he said, "That was the original."

"I still think it's good."

"I agree. But I want you to sing the refrain with me this time." He braced himself to hear her balk at his suggestion, but she surprised him by agreeing.

As she sang, their voices harmonized in a way he hadn't expected. He'd had a vibe about her talent, but he was convinced now. That song was meant to be a duet, and Connie was the only one who could do the female part justice.

Greg went on to sing the first verse, then asked, "What would you do with that?"

She thought for a moment, biting down on her bottom lip, then said, "Play it again."

When he did, she added her own twist to the melody, to the words, turning the song from romantic to sensual in a way that promised a sexual hint of things to come.

Dang. Her voice, the suggestive tone, turned him inside out. He'd never experienced foreplay in a song before.

When she finished, Greg set the guitar aside. "I haven't heard too many songs that made me want to make love, but damn, Connie. I..."

Their gazes met, and he realized words weren't necessary. A smoldering shadow of desire brewed in her eyes, and awareness dawned.

She'd been singing about him.

About *them*.

He reached for her jaw, his fingers extending to the back of her neck. As he drew her mouth to his, he expected her to stiffen, to pull back, to tell him he was out of line. Instead, she leaned forward and kissed him.

He wasn't sure what he was doing, where this was going, but if it stopped, she'd be calling the shots.

Her lips parted, and his tongue sought hers, dipping and tasting, giving and taking. Heat and hunger blindsided him, and he pulled her closer, deepening the kiss.

For a moment, he forgot where they were—*who* they were. All he could grasp was the raging desire, the demanding passion, the promise of something he'd never experienced before.

In the mind-soaring, world-tilting silence, music played in his head, an a cappella melody of hearts beating, hormones pumping, Christmas lights twinkling. The flickering flames in the fireplace joined in, as did the steady click of the clock on the mantel.

Surely, she heard it, too—the ensemble of arousal, the heat and desire.

There was only one thing to do.

Greg drew back, breaking their connection, then stood and reached out his hand, hoping she'd take it.

Connie, who was still reeling from the knee-weakening kiss, waited a beat before taking Greg's hand and allowing him to pull her to a stand.

For a moment, she thought he was going to lead her into the bedroom. And if he did, she wasn't at all sure what she'd say. What she'd do. It seemed as though her mind had completely deserted her once his lips touched hers.

But now, as they stood face-to-face, he didn't take her to bed. Instead, he drew her into his arms and began to sway in a slow and sensual dance. As she stepped into the rhythm and followed his lead, she fell captive to his musky scent, relishing a male embrace for the first time in what seemed like forever.

And it felt better than good.

It felt *right*.

She lifted her gaze until it met his. Then she touched his cheek, fingered his solid, square-cut jaw and the light bristle of a five-o'clock shadow.

Something surged between them, something hot and blood stirring. And she was afraid to move, afraid to breathe.

He placed his fingers over hers, where they rested on his cheek. Then he tilted her hand and dragged it to his mouth. As he brushed his lips across her palm, an erotic rush of goose bumps stole along her skin.

The warmth of his breath nearly buckled her knees, and she used her free hand to grab his shoulder and steady herself. He smiled, as though aware of the effect he had on her, then drew her mouth back to his.

As they kissed again, he moaned, and she whimpered.

Never had she experienced such a wild, demanding kiss. Never had she felt this kind of fire.

For a moment, she wanted to pull back. To tell him that they shouldn't mess around. That she wanted more for herself and the baby. Yet as her mom's voice rang in her ears, tossing out an I-told-you-so and words of caution, reminding her that a relationship with someone she wasn't married to would be wrong, her rebellious streak rallied.

Like she'd told her mom earlier today, it was her life, her choices, her consequences. And for whatever it was worth, making love with Greg didn't feel the least bit wrong.

Connie was a red-blooded woman with needs that hadn't been met in a long time. And even if she wanted more and this only proved to be a one-night thing, she didn't care. At this point, she was willing to settle for what little part of Greg he would give her.

Without warning, he pulled back, and she almost moaned in frustration. But he continued to hold her tight, his lips resting near her temple. "I don't have a condom."

"Neither do I," she admitted, her breath coming out in ragged little pants. "But we can check the bathroom drawer. There could be one in there."

"If not, I'll drive into Brighton Valley if I have to."

Connie left Greg in the living room and went to the bathroom, where she searched the medicine cabinet.

Nothing.

Then she checked the drawer and…bingo!

She wasn't sure who'd left the protection for them. It could have been Granny, she supposed. Or maybe it was Tori. It might have even been Fate. Either way, she wasn't going to worry about that now.

When she returned to the living room, a smile stretched across her face. "We're in luck." Then she reached for Greg's hand and led him to the small bedroom.

She placed the condom packet on the nightstand and turned back to face him.

He caught her cheeks with both hands. The intensity in his whiskey-brown gaze nearly took her breath away. If she'd had any second thoughts about taking their friendship to a sexual level, they faded in the pheromone-laden air.

"I want to make love to you more than anything," he said, "but I don't want to hurt you."

"You won't."

He kissed her again, and as their tongues continued to seek and savor, she tugged his shirttail out of his pants.

Following her lead, he unbuttoned his shirt and took it off. Then he removed his boots and pants.

After he'd bared himself, she slipped out of her robe and tossed it on the bed. Next, she gripped the fabric of her night-gown and slowly pulled it up and over her head. As the cotton fluttered to the floor, she stepped out of it and stood before him—naked.

Greg swallowed hard, transfixed at the sight of her. He could hardly believe the gift he'd been granted. In the past, he'd had women throw themselves at him, and he'd always taken it in stride. But Connie was different. And he suspected that he'd known it since the first day he'd met her.

"I...uh...I'm still a bit flabby. And I've got some stretch marks." She averted her eyes by glancing down at her bare feet.

He caught her chin with his finger and tilted her face so she looked at him. "You have a mother's heart, honey. So it's only natural that you'd have a mother's body. It only makes you more beautiful to me."

"That's so sweet. Thank you, Greg. I almost believe you."

"You'd better believe me because it's true."

She skimmed her fingers across his chest, sending a rush of heat through his blood. And for a moment, he closed his eyes, caught up in the magic of all he was feeling.

Then he drew her close, needing the skin-to-skin contact. Needing to feel her sweet body pressed against his.

His hands slid along the curve of her back, the slope of her hips, and a surge of passion slammed into him. Without thinking, he pulled her flush against him.

He meant to take it slow and easy, but when she arched forward, rubbing herself against his erection, he was lost. She threaded her fingers in his hair and gripped him with sexual desperation.

Passion flared, testosterone surged and the desire to make love to her nearly took his breath away. Unable to wait any longer, he scooped her up into his arms and placed her on the bed, where he stretched out next to her and continued to stroke, caress and kiss her senseless.

He'd never ached so badly to be inside of a woman before. But not just any woman.

This woman.

As her fingers brushed against his arousal, he shuddered with desire.

"I want you," she said. "Now."

"There's nothing I'd like more." He rolled to the side and hovered over her.

As she opened for him, he entered her slowly and gently. But when she arched up to meet him, when her body responded to his, they came together like star-crossed lovers who'd been given a second chance to make things right.

Greg increased the motion, taking and giving, until they both peaked. And as she cried out in a gripping release, he came in a star-shattering burst that seemed to illuminate the room.

They held tight on to each other until the ebbing waves of pleasure stilled.

Greg didn't know what tomorrow would bring, but tonight had been pure magic.

An hour later, after Connie had removed Amanda from her infant seat and put her into the crib, she'd returned to bed, where she and Greg lay amidst rumpled sheets.

She'd fallen asleep just moments ago, yet Greg had no desire to ever let her go. As he continued to hold her close, he savored the fragrance of her shampoo, the faint whiff of her peach scent.

Making love with Connie had been one of those once-in-a-lifetime experiences. A heart-stirring memory that would make him smile long after he went back on tour.

Of course, he still planned to take her with him. And now, with her bottom nestled in his lap and the scent of their love-making in the air, he was further convinced that he would have to talk her into going—one way or another.

He wished he had time to coax her, to work on her longer, but the clock was ticking. He'd have to come up with another way to convince her that her voice harmonized perfectly with his.

Suddenly, an idea came to him. An idea that just might work. All he had to do was call Gerald first thing in the morning.

If Greg couldn't take Connie to Nashville, then maybe he'd have to bring Nashville to her.

Chapter Ten

Since Connie had to work around Amanda's schedule, she sometimes had to prepare meals earlier than necessary. And this was one of those times.

While she waited for the men to come in for lunch, she sat at the kitchen table and thumbed through a magazine, scanning each article, each colorful picture. She tried to focus, but it was difficult to think about anything other than what she and Greg had done last night.

Up until then, Ross had been her only lover, and she'd had nothing to compare him to.

But now?

She didn't think she'd ever find a better lover than Greg.

Not that she wanted anyone else. Their lovemaking had surpassed her wildest dreams.

If there had ever been any doubts in her mind what she was feeling for him, there weren't any longer. She'd fallen in love with Greg, and while she hadn't told him outright, she'd sang the words to him.

Of course, now she was left to deal with all the after-the-loving questions, like "Where do we go from here?"

They hadn't had a chance to talk about that yet, although she suspected the answer was "Nowhere."

This morning, when she'd woken up in his arms, she'd realized the alarm hadn't gone off. Knowing that she had breakfast to prepare, she'd shot out of bed and hurried to the bathroom so she could shower and get dressed.

After she'd finished, she'd returned to the bedroom, only to find Greg talking on his cell phone. The conversation, as short-lived as it had been, seemed to be business related, which kind of surprised her. It was awfully early in the morning, no matter what time zone they were in.

Greg had ended the call shortly after she'd walked into the room, which had made her think that he might not have wanted her to be privy to talks about his upcoming tour.

Of course, his hanging up could have been a coincidence, she supposed. But even if it wasn't, she really couldn't blame him for not wanting to talk business in front of her. Yet after what they'd shared just hours before, she'd felt a bit…slighted.

She didn't mention anything, though. Instead, she'd fed Amanda, bundled her up, grabbed the diaper bag and took her to the ranch house so she could fix breakfast for everyone.

Granny had already started the coffee, thank goodness.

As Connie buzzed about the kitchen, trying to play catch-up, she'd sensed that everyone knew what she and Greg had done and why she'd been late.

Unable to help herself, she apologized to Granny and the men, blaming the baby, who'd actually slept better last night than she ever had.

Now that Connie was no longer rushed and breakfast was over, she couldn't help thinking about Greg again, about what they'd shared last night. And she couldn't help wondering what would become of them. She suspected that things would end the minute he left on tour—if not before—and the realization clawed at her heart.

She had no one to blame but herself, though. Before getting sexually involved, she'd known that their lives were worlds apart. And that a relationship could never be lasting.

But she'd made a conscious choice and would live with the consequences, no matter how much they hurt.

Flipping through the magazine pages, she continued to skim the photographs and articles until a spread about Southwestern cooking caught her eye.

Maybe she would try her hand at making enchiladas for dinner one of these nights. Connie, like most people who'd grown up in Texas, loved Mexican food.

Come to think of it, though, that was one of the few specialties her mother shied away from.

Not that Dinah didn't like tacos and such. She did. But she'd never gotten the hang of creating the flavorful sauces of the dishes she found so appealing.

Besides, her viewers, who were predominately Anglo, tended to be the steak-and-potatoes type. So, for that reason, fair-haired

Dinah took back her maiden name, thinking it would be more appropriate.

It really hadn't been an ethnocentric decision, though. If truth be known, she loved Mexican people and their culture. After all, she'd married Connie's dad, Ricardo Montoya, and had bore him two children.

As Connie continued to scan the article, she noticed a recipe for fajitas. It looked easy enough. Maybe she'd try it next week.

Spotting an insert that offered a thirty-day free trial for a Southwestern-style cookbook, she tore out the mail-in postcard without giving it much thought and shoved it into her pocket to fill out later.

Footsteps crunched on the back porch as Greg entered the house, and her heart skipped a beat.

She watched him hang his hat on a hook in the mudroom.

"Hey," he said, as he strode into the kitchen, closing the gap between them. He brushed a kiss on her cheek. "Something sure smells good."

"Thanks." She'd only recently started getting compliments on her meals, so she offered him a genuine smile. "I made fried chicken for lunch."

He headed to the sink, then washed his hands.

She noted that he didn't look the least bit dirty or sweaty. "What have you been up to?"

Once the words were out, she nearly winced. She sure hoped he didn't think she was getting territorial; she'd just been curious, that's all.

"I went to the drugstore." He flashed her a boyish grin. "I had some things to stock up on."

Condoms?

She sure hoped so, but not for the reason he might think. If he'd picked up more protection, it meant that last night hadn't been a onetime thing.

Of course, that didn't mean that they would continue a relationship once he went on tour.

Again her heart ached at the thought of letting go. She'd known whatever they had wouldn't last, but that didn't make it easier to imagine him packing up his things and driving off.

"Have you given any more thought about going on tour with me and the band?" he asked. "Hearing you sing last night convinced me that you're just what I've been looking for. So the audition isn't really necessary."

"I told you that I wasn't interested."

"Yeah, I know. But I thought that after last night, you might reconsider."

She crossed her arms and furrowed her brow. "I hope you weren't trying to seduce me into changing my mind."

"Hey, what kind of guy do you think I am? Sweet-talking you into a business arrangement last night was the furthest thing on my mind." He closed the gap between them and placed his hands on her shoulders. Then he leaned over and brushed a kiss across her cheek. "I just thought that…well, that it might be nice to have someone warm my bed when I'm on the road."

"I'm sure you have plenty of 'someones' who'd love to do that." She'd meant that as a tongue-in-cheek response, yet the truth of that statement didn't sit well with her.

He gave her shoulders a squeeze, before releasing her. "Maybe I'm not interested in anyone else."

Her heart wrapped itself around hope, but she knew better than to put too much stock into it. Men like Greg Clayton didn't give up their fame and careers to be husbands and daddies.

She closed the magazine and set it aside. Then she stood and made her way to the stove to check on the potatoes that had been baking.

"Are you nervous about being onstage?" he asked.

"No, that's not it." She reached into a drawer and pulled out a fork. Then she turned to face Greg. "My mother is Dinah Rawlings, and I'm afraid she's the showman in my family."

"Dinah Rawlings?" His brow furrowed. "I'm sorry, but I don't know who that is."

It seemed as though everyone knew Dinah, but Connie realized men like Greg might not be familiar with her at all. "She has a syndicated television show that appeals to women."

"You mean, *In the Kitchen with Dinah?*"

So he had at least heard of the show.

She nodded. "That's the one. And her career and her television shows were a huge part of her life while I was growing up. Too huge. And I refuse to put my job or career ahead of my daughter like she did. I just want a quiet life."

Surely Greg could understand that.

She returned to her task, opening the oven door then poking one of the potatoes with a fork. It was still too hard.

After closing the oven and setting the fork aside, she turned to face him again. "Don't you get tired of it? The traveling? Sleeping in strange beds? The constant buzz of excitement?" She would think that, after a while, it would get old.

"No, I'll never get tired of it. I get a real rush being onstage.

It's the one place where I know that I've finally made it." Greg pulled out a chair and sat at the table. "My biological mother had high hopes for me. And I like thinking that she's looking down from heaven and that she's proud of the man I became."

"You know, I really don't have anything against fame. Or performing. But it was tough growing up with a mother who was consumed by her TV show ratings and her career."

"I'm sorry you had to go through that," he said.

"It wasn't always bad," she admitted. "When my dad was alive and my mother had stayed home to take care of Becky and me, we were happy. But then things changed, and I had to spend most of my time with nannies and housekeepers."

"When did you hook up with that band?"

"I left home when I turned eighteen. And a year later, I met some band members at this place where I used to hang out. When they found out I could sing, they asked me to join them. I have to admit that it was fun. At least, sometimes. But part of the appeal was that I knew my mom hated what I was doing. She really flipped when she learned that I was singing for my supper and insisted that I 'stop that nonsense' and come home immediately."

"I take it that you didn't."

"No. Actually, I liked being onstage, even if my life wasn't quite as glamorous as my mother's."

She'd had to remind herself that it hadn't been a competition. Yet a small voice suggested that it probably was back then. At least, a little bit.

"Is lunch ready?" Granny asked, as she entered the kitchen.

"Almost." Connie pointed to the oven. "I'm waiting on the potatoes. It'll just be a minute or two longer."

"How do you feel about going out on the town with me tonight?" Greg asked.

Connie took a seat next to him. "What have you got in mind?"

"I thought it would be fun for us to go to the Buckshot Inn."

Connie furrowed her brow. "What's that?"

"It's a little hole-in-the-wall place just outside Brighton Valley city limits," Granny explained. "Greg got his start there, and each time he's back in town, he makes a surprise appearance."

"I'm sure Granny wouldn't mind babysitting," Greg said. "And we don't have to stay long."

"I'd love to watch Amanda for you," Granny said. "I think it would be good for you to get out and have some fun."

Connie probably ought to pass on a night out, but she'd spent the last nine months holed up on the ranch. And while she'd found safety and comfort here, she looked forward to going somewhere, even if it was just to a local watering hole.

"It does sound fun," she admitted, deciding to let down her guard for just one night.

Who would recognize her there?

The Buckshot Inn sat on the edge of the county road, flanked by a scrap-metal recycling yard on one side and a field of grazing cattle on the other.

Granny had been right to call it a hole-in-the-wall, Connie decided, since it wasn't very big. But it was definitely a local hot spot. The place was buzzing with activity, something Connie easily surmised after noting the number of cars, pickups and motorcycles that filled the graveled parking lot.

To find an empty spot, Greg had to drive around to the back, where the only space available was next to a battered green Dumpster. As they climbed out of the rental car, he reached for his guitar. Then they made their way to the front of the building, where a pink neon Open sign hung in a window trimmed with blinking red-and-green Christmas lights.

When they reached the entrance, Greg opened the door, and Connie stepped inside.

Laughter and chatter competed with the band that was playing their own rendition of a Randy Travis song. They were giving it their best shot, but they weren't doing Randy or the song justice. Still, it didn't seem to matter. Everyone appeared to be having a good time anyway.

Connie scanned the interior as they looked for a place to sit. With its scarred hardwood floors and honky-tonk decor, the Buckshot Inn wasn't much different than any of the places at which the South Forty used to play, but it appeared to be a whole lot more popular.

A balding, fifty-something man came up to Greg almost immediately and reached out his hand in greeting. "Good to see you again. I heard you were back in town."

"Thanks, Mel. It's good to be home." Greg then introduced Melvin Draper as the owner of the Buckshot Inn.

"I see you brought your guitar," Melvin said. "My patrons always love it when you treat us to a song or two."

"It only seems right to stop in and pay my respects. You gave me a chance to prove myself, and I'll never forget that."

Mel laughed. "It really wasn't much of a gamble, son. You have more talent in your little pinky than most guys have in their entire right arm. And that first time you played and sang for me,

I knew you'd go all the way to the top—if you were willing to make it happen."

Connie couldn't agree more with Melvin about Greg's talent, but she kept her glowing praise to herself.

"Let's find a table," Greg said.

Connie followed Greg toward a booth near the far wall. But it wasn't easy. He continued to stop along the way and say hello to several of the Buckshot regulars.

When he spotted an older man dressed in a bright red Western shirt with the top buttons undone, he said, "Hey, Gerald. I'm glad you made it."

The man wore a black Stetson, but it couldn't hide a full head of white curly hair. A gold chain with a medallion hung from his neck and rested against his bare chest.

Greg paused to shake hands. Then he introduced him as Gerald Grainger. His two companions were a young man named Hank and a lanky, dark-haired guy named Joe.

"Thanks for coming," Greg told the men.

"We wouldn't have missed this for the world. Isn't that right, Hank?" He smiled at the younger men, one of whom would probably get carded if he ordered a beer.

"If you'll excuse us," Greg said, "I want to get a table before they're all taken. I'll come back and talk to you later."

The men nodded in agreement, but they both seemed intrigued by Connie. In fact, as they zeroed in on her, she wondered if she'd forgotten to zip her black jeans or if she'd lost a button on her pink blouse.

She shrugged off their interest, though. They were probably just trying to figure out her connection to Greg.

When they were finally seated in the booth, Greg motioned for the cocktail waitress, a matronly woman with a ready smile.

"Hi there," she said, as she whipped out a notepad. "What'll y'all have?"

Connie ordered a ginger ale, and Greg asked for a Corona and lime.

Ten minutes later, the band announced that they were taking a break, and Greg reached for his guitar.

As some of the crowd noticed what he was doing, they began to clap and cheer. Once he reached the microphone, it took him several minutes to quiet them down.

"Thanks for the warm welcome," he said, his voice booming through the room. "I hope you don't mind if I sing a couple of songs for you—for old time's sake. You see, Melvin Draper decided to take a chance on me when I was just out of high school and still ordering soda pops. And that's something I'll never forget."

Someone in the rear whistled, then said, "We ain't ever gonna forget you, either, Greg."

As he strummed a few chords, the crowd settled down again, waiting to hear what he had to say.

"You folks from Brighton Valley are like family. So I'd like to share a couple of my favorite tunes." He then launched into a hit that was fast becoming a standard in honky-tonks everywhere. And when he'd finished to the boot-stomping roar of the audience, he sang another about a rodeo cowboy who'd given up everything for fame.

Again, the cheers went up.

"I've got one last song for you tonight," Greg said. "And

since the Buckshot launched my career, it seems only fitting that you folks hear it first."

Again, the fellow in back let out a whoop and a whistle.

"Connie?" Greg said, his voice sounding deep yet hesitant. He reached out his hand toward her. "Come up here and help me do this right."

Her heart dropped to the pit of her stomach. Was he crazy? She waved him off and shook her head no.

"Aw, come on, honey. You've got a voice as pretty as a honky-tonk angel's. And there isn't anyone else who can do it right."

She felt her resolve buckle, and she tried to shore it up. But he was right. She knew how good that song was when they sang it together. It wouldn't have the same effect as a solo.

The crowd began to clap and cheer, egging her on.

She ought to refuse, to pay Greg back for putting her on the spot. Yet something deep inside of her wanted to help him launch that song.

Ever so slowly, she slid out of the booth and got to her feet. Then she made her way to the stage.

She slid him a You're-going-to-be-sorry-for-this look.

His eyes glimmered, and a rebellious smile stretched across his face, as he whispered, "I'll make it up to you."

He could count on that, she thought, trying to ignore the tingle that shot up her spine at the heat in his gaze.

As he began to strum the guitar, a hush spread through the crowd. It was almost as though every one of them knew they were going to hear something special. As though they believed that history was being made tonight.

And maybe it was.

As he'd done back at the cabin, Greg opened with the first verse, and she joined in for the second.

For the next minute or two, she and Greg were the only ones in the room. Caught up in the music, in the slow and sensual beat, they sang the words as though they meant every single one.

And as far as Connie was concerned, she did.

Excitement rushed through her veins, but it had nothing to do with the performance and everything to do with the way Greg was looking at her now.

As the last lyrics were sung, as the last chord sounded, Greg leaned forward and kissed her, sweetly, thoroughly.

And when it was all over—the song, the long, sensual kiss— the crowd jumped to their feet, whooping it up and giving them a standing ovation.

"I knew it," Greg said.

"Knew what?"

"That they were going to love you."

"It's the song," she argued.

"It's more that that." He reached out and gave her hand a squeeze.

Connie's heart was pumping, and her mind was spinning, and the applause was echoing in her ears.

Something told her that no matter what "it" was, no matter what had just happened, her life was never going to be the same again.

Chapter Eleven

As he held Connie's hand and listened to the crowd's reaction to the duet they'd just sang, Greg's heart thundered in his chest. For once, as he stood onstage, he felt more than pride in a job well done.

Something mesmerizing had just happened, and he'd been a part of it.

The audience wasn't just clapping and cheering because of the words or the music he'd written. Or because of the sound of his voice or the way it had melded with Connie's.

The song had been so moving, the words and feelings so real, that a couple of people were wiping tears from their eyes.

Greg gave Connie's hand another squeeze, trying to convey all he felt. All he dreamed.

Her smile and the gleam in her eyes told him that she knew

they'd really connected with the audience tonight. And that it was more than just their onstage chemistry and an ability to harmonize.

It was clear to him that she wasn't sorry he'd put her on the spot. Not after the fact. And that she was feeling the rush, too.

As they made their way toward the booth where they'd been sitting, Gerald intercepted them. He was grinning like a rat that had outfoxed a barn cat. "Damn, Greg. You weren't kidding. That song is going to fly to the top of the charts. And that little lady will be a great addition to the show."

Connie stiffened.

"I get paid to know these things," Gerald added. "And I'd bet the farm against a stale doughnut that you've got a major hit on your hands."

"Greg?" Connie asked. "Who is this guy?"

"Gerald Grainger is my manager." Greg realized she might not be happy to hear that he'd set her up to play for a special audience, but Gerald had a gift when it came to talking people into things, which was one reason Greg had hired him. Besides, Greg was hoping that Gerald could do what he hadn't been able to: convince Connie to join them on the winter tour.

Anger flared in her eyes, and she crossed her arms over her chest. "Let me set you straight, Mr. Grainger. I'm not going anywhere. And I'm not singing onstage."

"You haven't heard how much we're prepared to offer you."

"Whatever it is, I'm not interested." She gave Greg a frown bursting with disappointment, then pushed her way through the crowd and headed for the booth where they'd been sitting.

Greg lifted his Stetson, raked a hand through his hair then

adjusted the hat back on his head. He'd assumed that once she got onstage and heard the crowd's approval, when she felt the addictive rush, she'd be just as eager to record and perform the song as he was. And that she'd agree to go on tour, even if it was just for the winter months.

Whenever Greg wanted something, he made it happen. And whether it was to run away from a Mexican orphanage when he was twelve, to score the winning touchdown on the high school football field or to reach the limelight onstage, he'd always been driven to succeed.

But this was different. Convincing Connie to go on tour with him was proving to be his biggest challenge yet. And so far, he'd failed miserably.

He should have known that orchestrating something like this would upset her, and he wasn't sure what to do about it now.

Apologize?

Something told him it wasn't going to be that simple.

Maybe he'd been wrong to even try. But how was he supposed to back down now?

Gerald slapped a hand on Greg's shoulder. "I gotta tell you. I thought you were just blowing smoke, but you weren't kidding. That little gal is perfect."

That she was.

And in more ways than one.

"She's got the voice I was looking for," was all Greg was willing to admit at this point.

"She's a winner, that's for sure. But it's more than her talent shining through." Gerald winked at Greg and grinned. "She was singing her heart out tonight."

"What do you mean?"

"That little gal was singing to *you*. And she meant every last word that came out of her mouth."

For a moment, Greg felt like an adolescent discussing his latest crush in the boy's locker room.

No kidding? Dude. Do you think she really likes me?

Yet if Gerald was right, and Connie was falling for him, there'd be a slew of problems.

She was looking for a family man. A man who worked a nine-to-five job and who would come home each night. And Greg Clayton could never be that man.

"The thing is," Gerald added, "it wasn't just Connie making that song work. I saw the way you looked at her—like she crossed your eyes and curled your toes, too. That kind of chemistry doesn't just happen."

Greg wanted to object, to tell Gerald he was all wet. That he was dreaming.

But Connie *had* done something to him; he just wasn't prepared to deal with whatever it was. Or to make that kind of compromise. He thrived on touring the country, and she was content to hole up in Brighton Valley.

"You got that possum in the headlights look," Gerald said, chuckling. "Love or lust or whatever you're feeling for each other isn't a bad thing. We'll make it work to our benefit."

Greg wasn't so sure he wanted to "make it work." At least, not up onstage. What he and Connie shared had been both natural and personal. And not something to flaunt to all the world.

Of course, right now, their relationship—whatever it was—had suffered a serious blow.

He glanced toward the booth, only to see that Connie wasn't sitting there.

Uh-oh. He placed a hand on Gerald's shoulder. "Listen, I've got to go. Talking her into going on tour with me just got a whole lot harder than I expected."

"Why's that?"

"She just took off. And I think she's planning to go home without me."

"Don't let her get away."

Greg didn't intend to.

"By the way," Gerald added as Greg started toward the door. "I've got a marketing strategy for that song, and it's going to start at a grassroots level."

"Whatever," Greg said, as he tried to catch up with Connie.

Right now, Gerald's game plan didn't interest him in the least.

As soon as Connie had gotten back to the table, she'd grabbed her purse and started toward the door.

When she'd been involved with Ross, he'd tried to manipulate her every chance he got. And she'd be darned if she would let Greg use the same tactics. She might have been young and foolish once, but she wasn't going to let history repeat itself.

As she made her way to the door, she spotted a big, burly guy about six-foot-six and weighing at least 250 pounds. He was standing near the door with his hands on his hips.

She didn't have to ask if he worked here or what his job was. His forearms rivaled Popeye's and his biceps stretched the sleeves of a red T-shirt. White letters across his chest said: THE BUCKSHOT INN—The Ruckus Stops Here.

"Excuse me," Connie said to the man she assumed was a bouncer. "Can you please call me a cab?"

"Sure thing, ma'am." He grabbed his cell phone and began to dial.

She glanced back at the crowd, only to see Greg approaching.

"Hey." He reached for her arm in an attempt to get her attention.

While the move wasn't rough or abrupt, it was too Ross-like for Connie's comfort, and she twisted and pulled out of his grip.

Yet unlike the response she would have expected from Ross, Greg's hand dropped to his side. "What are you doing?"

She lifted her chin, determined not to let him stop her. "I'm leaving."

"Okay. As soon as I pay the tab, we'll go."

"You go ahead and stay with your friends. I'm taking a cab."

"That's not necessary." He reached into his pocket, pulled out his money clip and peeled off a couple of twenties. Then he handed the cash to the bouncer. "Would you please take care of my tab for me? And while you're at it, cancel that cab."

"Sure thing, Mr. Clayton." The guy beamed as though he'd been blessed with the task.

"I'm sorry," Greg told Connie. "I messed up—big-time. And I don't blame you for being mad. But there's no point in your taking a cab. I'm ready to go."

She wanted to object, to tell him to take a flying leap off the Tallahassee Bridge, but she was in a hurry to escape, and she wasn't up for a scene. So she reluctantly agreed.

Greg pushed open the door for her, and they headed for the

car. When he unlocked the door, they both climbed in and drove to the ranch in silence.

Ten minutes later, Greg parked in front of the house. Connie started to get out, and he stopped her. "Don't go in yet. We need to talk about this."

"There's not much to say." She didn't see any reason for a lengthy discussion. He'd apologized, and she'd made her point.

Trying to come up with some kind of compromise would be fruitless. She and Greg obviously lived in different worlds. And even though she loved him, she wasn't going to leave her world for his.

Besides, whenever she and Ross would have a fight, he thought that sex was a great peacemaker. So she wasn't going to let Greg get within ten feet of the bedroom in the cabin until after they'd reached some kind of agreement. And she wasn't at that place yet.

"I made a big mistake," Greg admitted. "I didn't mean to back you into a corner. And I didn't mean to disregard your feelings." He reached across the console and took her hand in his. "I'm sorry, honey."

She felt her body buckle at his touch, but she was determined to be strong. After all, she'd given in to Ross too often. And she was determined to think this through.

"I'm mad," she told Greg, "but I'll get over it. At least, I think I'll get over it, as long as you'll back off and stop trying to make me go on the road with you. But right now, I just want some time alone."

"Okay. I'll give you the time to cool off and think about it. But I want you to know that Amanda is important to me, too. So I should have been more considerate, and I apologize for that. If you don't want to come on tour, that's fine. I'll look for someone else. But I'll tell you right now, there's no one else I'd rather work with."

She found it difficult to remain angry with him, even if she was still hurt and reeling from his deception. "I accept your apology."

"No harm done?" he asked.

She supposed not. Especially since Ross would never get wind of this and find out where she was. And to make sure that didn't happen, she figured Greg would need to understand why she couldn't agree to go onstage with him ever again.

"No, I'm sure it's okay, but there's something I probably ought to tell you." She took a deep breath and slowly blew it out. "I got involved with a guy more than a year ago, and things got…ugly."

"Was that Amanda's father?" Greg asked.

"Yes. His name was Ross."

Greg caressed the top of her hand with his thumb. "You told me that he was a jerk."

"He was nice when I met him, and he kept prodding me to sing with the band. I agreed, but then I started getting more attention than he counted on. He was a jealous man. And when he drank, he morphed into a brute."

Greg tensed, his brow furrowed and his thumb grew still. "Did he hurt you?"

"Yes." She glanced down at the floorboard, not proud of the memories. "It started with a push and a shove. Then one day, he actually hit me. I told him it had better not happen again, and he swore it wouldn't."

"Did it? Did he hit you a second time?"

"I shouldn't have stayed with him, but like a fool, I believed him when he cried and told me how sorry he was. But it had all been a lie. A couple of days later, he saw me talking to a guy. It was totally innocent, but Ross had been downing shots of tequila, and he flipped out. That time, he didn't just hit me, he beat me. And when the police arrived, I pressed charges."

"Good for you."

She blew out a sigh, ready to level with him completely, no matter how stupid she felt. "When Ross was arrested, he threatened to come looking for me and to make me pay for what I'd done."

"Oh, God," Greg said. "Have you been hiding out from him?"

"Yes. He doesn't know about the baby, and I'd like to keep it that way."

Greg gripped her hand and pulled it to his mouth, then he pressed a kiss into her palm. "You don't have to worry about him ever again, Connie. I'll hire bodyguards to protect you. In fact, I'll tell everyone the baby is mine."

"That's sweet of you," she said.

"In fact," he said, drawing closer, "we could even get married. That way, he'll know he has to stay away from you."

As much as she'd grown to love Greg, as much as she hated to admit that she'd harbored a crazy dream of them working through their differences, his proposal fell flat.

She couldn't possibly marry a man for all the wrong reasons. "Thanks for the offer, Greg, but marriage is out of the question. And I won't go on tour."

"Whatever you say." He seemed a bit more relieved than disappointed. Still, he pressed another kiss on her fingers. "Come on, let's go get Amanda and take her to bed."

As much as she wanted to curl up beside Greg, to make use of those condoms he'd bought and to put tonight behind them, she refused to use sex as a balm. Or to let it work as a pair of blinders. The next time she got seriously involved with a man, it would be with both eyes open.

"You can walk us to the door," she said, "but I think it's best if we sleep separately tonight."

"Better for whom?" he asked.

"For me."

Yet somewhere deep inside, she wasn't so sure.

Connie tossed and turned all night, her thoughts torn between desperately wanting to work things out with Greg and wanting to end things before she was inconsolably hurt.

Greg cared about her—of that she had no doubt. But he didn't love her. At least, he hadn't mentioned it. He had, of course, apologized—and it had seemed sincere, which caused her to question why she'd insisted upon sleeping alone in the first place.

Yet she couldn't imagine waiting months on end for him to return to the Rocking C so they could see each other again. Nor could she imagine knowing he would spend the bulk of his time away from home, flocked by a bevy of groupies eager to ease his loneliness and warm his bed.

With each time she rolled to one side or the other and plumped her pillow, she'd tried to find a solution or a compromise. But so far, she hadn't been able to come up with one she considered viable.

At four in the morning, Amanda woke up starving and completely oblivious to the trouble her mom had been wrestling with all night long.

Connie nursed her, then showered and got ready to face the day. She still hadn't made a decision about what to do, though. The way she saw it, she could have a part of Greg—while he was at the Rocking C. But being a part-time lover wasn't something she would settle for. She deserved so much more than that.

And Amanda deserved a full-time daddy.

So there it was. She'd pondered the situation all night long and still didn't have a solution.

After bundling up the baby and placing her in the carrier, Connie headed for the house. When she entered the back door, she found Greg sitting at the kitchen table. He was dressed in faded blue jeans and a black T-shirt. His hair was damp, so she suspected he'd showered. But he didn't appear to have slept any better than she had.

She couldn't help thinking that, like her, he'd struggled with the same lousy options and come up with the same lame solutions. And that he might even be as miserable about the mess as she was.

"Good morning." He flashed her a heart-strumming smile and got to his feet. "The coffee's ready."

"Thank you."

He reached for Amanda, and Connie passed her to him. Yet instead of using the time to get busy, she watched the two people she loved most in the world and fought the urge to embrace them both. To tell Greg that they could indeed find a way around their differences.

Instead, she took a flat of eggs and several packages of

sausage out of the refrigerator. As she started breakfast, she listened to Greg coo and talk to the baby. *"Aw, preciosa, que linda."*

Her heart waffled again. There was so much to love about him, so much to admire.

She just wished that he somehow could become the man she needed him to be, but she knew that—even if he wanted to—he could never give up his career. And she would never ask him to. Performing was such a vital part of who he was.

So where did that leave them?

Nowhere. Connie wasn't ever going to juggle her life and her dreams around someone's career again, which meant that she was back to square one with no solution in sight.

So she focused on her work, going through the motions as she scrambled eggs and fried links of sausage. Then she fed the men breakfast, as she'd done each morning since she'd moved in.

Around ten o'clock, when it was time for Amanda's nap, she returned to the cabin, her heart heavier than it had ever been. She struggled to count her blessings and forget her worries, but that was easier said than done.

She nursed the baby, then put her in the crib. She watched her for a moment before leaving her to sleep, but a heavy heart continued to drag her down.

Once back in the living room, her gaze lit upon the tree in the corner. Without the lights turned on, it looked dull and lifeless—a fir that had been cut down before its prime.

Connie couldn't help but think that the same could be said about her.

Today was Christmas Eve, and while she tried to reach deep inside of herself, she just couldn't find an ounce of the holiday spirit.

She strode to the corner, then bent to plug in the lights, wishing it was that easy to illuminate her heart. She'd no more than stood upright when the telephone rang, and she snatched it from the cradle. "Hello?"

Rather than a greeting or an introduction, her mother lapsed right into her reason for the call. "I thought you weren't singing anymore. You told me you were cooking at a ranch. Why did you lie to me? I could have handled the truth."

"What are you talking about?" Connie asked. "I didn't lie."

"I turned on the news this morning, and a reporter who does a special called Celebrity Secrets said that you would be going on tour this winter with a famous country singer. I can't remember which one off the top of my head, although I'd heard his name before."

"Slow down," Connie said. "I'm not following you."

"According to the reporter, you've been singing in honky-tonks again."

"That's not true," Connie said.

"The clip was supposed to have been filmed last night."

No way. Connie hadn't seen a camera crew. "That's impossible. I did sing last night, but it was only one song."

"Your hair is much shorter than it used to be," her mother added.

Connie still struggled with the news. "Are you sure about this?"

"I'm just telling you what I saw. It appeared to be a homemade video recording of you singing at someplace called the Longshot or the Buckshot. They called it a club, but from the looks of the place, it was just a backwoods bar."

"Oh, my God." Connie ran a hand through her hair. "It was totally impromptu. And it was just one song."

"It was actually a great song, and the audience went wild."

Connie plopped down in the recliner. "I can't believe this."

"Well, you can see it for yourself. It wasn't a professional recording. Someone taped it on a camcorder or something. But it's getting a lot of buzz. They're saying the song is destined to be a hit."

"I had no idea…"

"The reporter said that it was posted on YouTube, as well as the singer's Web site. So if you want to see it for yourself, you can check it out."

"I believe you. It's just that I… Well, I can't understand who would have…"

"It must have been that country star. Let me think. Who was it? Oh, yes. Greg Clayton." Her mom blew out a sigh. "I realize he's not a nobody like Ross. But that's not the point. I'm hurt that you felt you had to lie to me."

Connie's stomach lurched. "I haven't been lying, Mom. I've been living on a ranch near Brighton Valley. And for the first time since I moved in and started working here, I went out. Greg insisted that I join him onstage. And it was only one song…."

How could Greg do that to her? Put her on display and make everything so…public? Especially after their talk… After she'd told him about hiding out from Ross.

God. She felt betrayed. Deceived.

"I'm not familiar with Greg Clayton's music, but from what

I heard, he has a nice voice—very sexy, actually. I picked up a hint of his accent…." Her mom sighed, and her tone grew almost wistful. "It reminded me of the way your father used to talk and the way… Well, it brought back a few memories is all."

Yeah, Connie was digging up a memory of her own. How that sexy Latin cowboy had betrayed her.

"I'd just hoped you would find someone other than a musician," her mom said. "Someone different than Ron."

"His name is *Ross*." Connie, who was still trying to sort through what was happening to her and what she was going to do about it, had half a notion to insist to her mother that Greg was absolutely nothing like Ross. They were from different planets, if you actually compared them. But they'd both hurt her. And while Greg had never laid a hand on her that wasn't sweet and gentle, he'd crushed her just the same.

Oh, dear God. What if Ross saw the tape? What if he was able to track her down?

"Listen, Mom. I need to hang up now, but I'll talk to you later today. Will you be home?"

"Yes. I have a couple of last-minute gifts to buy, but I should be back around two."

"Good. I'm coming home for Christmas after all."

"That's great, but I thought you had to work."

"No, something unexpected came up, and I'm taking time off." A *lot* of time.

Connie didn't like bailing out on Granny, but if anyone understood, it would be her.

When the call ended, Connie went to the bedroom and packed up everything she could in a single suitcase; traveling with a baby was going to be hard enough. Then she called the ranch house to give Granny the news about the airing of that tape and her decision to leave.

"I'm sorry to leave you in a bind at Christmas, Granny, but I can't risk letting Ross find me."

"I understand, honey. Where are you going? Can you at least drop me a line and let me know where you'll be?"

"I'm going to spend Christmas with my mother. I've got a gift that's going to surprise her conservative socks off. And after that, I'm not sure where I'll go."

"All right. Why don't I ask Earl to give you a ride into Houston?"

"I hate to put you or him out."

"Oh, pshaw. It's the least I can do for you." Granny clicked her tongue. "You know, I still can't believe Greg would be a party to tricking you like that."

"He must have been. That homemade video is on his Web site." Or so she'd been told. She hadn't taken time to find out for sure. But why would her mother lie?

"Have you talked to Greg about this?" Granny asked.

"No. Is he there?" Connie hoped he was. She'd give him a piece of her mind before leaving.

"I'm afraid he left around nine o'clock this morning and drove into Houston. He said he had some shopping to do."

Shopping around that video, no doubt.

Connie refused to let Greg's desire for success and stardom affect her and Amanda—no matter how much she'd come to care about him, no matter how much she'd grown to love him.

She'd made a lot of mistakes in recent years, but she was going to do things right from here on out.

First she would confront her mother and tell her the truth about Ross and the baby. Then she would take off for parts unknown.

And this time, she wouldn't tell anyone where she was.

Chapter Twelve

Greg returned from the city just before noon and carried a small shopping bag into the house. He'd done a lot of thinking over the past twelve hours and had come to a decision. He had to make it up to Connie for pressing her to get onstage last night.

He suspected that she'd been okay with performing at first, while they'd been singing. It wasn't until Gerald had introduced himself and mentioned going on tour that she'd gotten upset.

"Don't let her get away," Gerald had told Greg at the Buckshot Inn.

Greg hadn't needed any advice. He was going to do whatever he could to make her happy. After that, he would go on tour with whatever backup singer Gerald could find. And then he'd cut back on his schedule for the rest of the year.

Maybe Connie would agree to that. He hoped so, because he

wanted her and the baby to be a permanent part of his life, which was why he'd thrown out a proposal last night.

In all honesty, the idea had just rolled out of his mouth, but the more he thought about it, the more he realized it wasn't all that wild. In fact, marriage just might solve all of their problems—her need for protection and his need for... Well, for *her*. She hadn't been interested, though, which had him a bit puzzled.

As Greg entered the house, he caught a whiff of something baking in the oven.

Meat loaf maybe? It sure smelled good.

Assuming that Connie was cooking, he went into the kitchen, eager to talk to her. He might even decide to give her an early Christmas present, one that shouldn't wait one more day.

But it was Granny who stood over the stove, lifting a lid and peeking into a pot.

"Where's Connie?" he asked.

"She's gone."

He strode for the cookie jar for a snack to tide him over until lunch was on the table. "When will she be back?"

His mother turned slowly and crossed her arms over her chest. "She won't be coming back, Greg. She gave me her resignation this morning."

"What?" The unexpected news slammed into Greg and spun his heart a full three-sixty. "You're kidding. Where did she go?"

"I'm not sure, but after what you did to her, I can't say that I blame her."

"You mean pushing her to go onstage last night?"

"No, I think she would have been okay with that. But you

shouldn't have let anyone tape her singing and then broadcast it all over the country."

Greg's pulse rate skidded to a halt as he grappled with the hit-and-run version of events. "What are you talking about?"

"You didn't know?"

"No."

Granny must have read the shock and the sincerity in his expression and realized he was truly clueless, because she did him a favor and explained. "Someone had a camera of some kind at the Buckshot Inn last night. And apparently, the clip is already on the Internet and on your Web site."

"Oh, crap." He leaned his hip against the kitchen counter, floored by the news.

Is that what Gerald had meant about a grassroots plan?

"Connie had a very good reason for wanting to keep a low profile," his mother added.

His heart sunk to the pit of his stomach. Oh, God. If that guy—Ross—found Connie, if he so much as said one word to her...

Greg looked at his mother, his gaze latching onto hers like a drowning man reaching for a buoy. "I didn't know anything about this. You have to believe me."

"I'm glad to hear that. I didn't think you'd stoop to something so low, but I know how driven you can be when you want something."

She said it like being focused and determined was a bad thing, and he couldn't agree. "I'm not *that* driven."

"Either way, you'd better do something."

Of that he was sure. "I'll find her, Granny."

"And then what?"

Hell if he knew.

His mother placed a hand on his forearm and gave it a loving squeeze. "Connie needs someone to look after her and the baby. Someone who's not on the road ten months out of the year."

"Are you suggesting I give up my career?"

"No. But maybe it's become a bigger priority in your life than it ought to be. Marriage means compromise."

Marriage? Had Connie told his mom that he'd proposed to her? He hadn't asked her the way he should have—if he'd put some time and thought into it.

Is that why she'd declined? Because he hadn't dropped to one knee and offered chocolates and flowers, too?

Or was there another reason?

When she'd sung that duet with him, she'd actually sung *to* him. It's what had made that song and their performance so magical. And if truth be told, he'd felt the evidence of her love, even before Gerald had mentioned it.

He just hadn't wanted to believe it.

Of course, she hadn't actually told him she loved him, even when they'd made love.

So what had Connie and his mother talked about? And how had the "M" word come up?

There was always the chance that Connie hadn't mentioned it at all. Granny was on a big matchmaking kick, especially since Jared and Matt had both bit the matrimonial bullet. So it's possible she'd just imagined that Connie would consider marriage.

Greg blew out a ragged breath. The trouble was, regardless

of how Connie felt about him, about *them,* he felt a hole as big as Texas in his chest. It seemed as if he'd lost…his family.

"Where can I find her?" he asked.

"She took the baby to her mother's. But don't dally, son. She plans to disappear after Christmas."

Greg wasn't going to drag his boots.

He was going to get his family and bring them home.

Dinah Rawlings and her oldest daughter lived in an impressive brick home in the Woodlands, an exclusive, high-class area of Houston that was tucked away in a forest of trees and shrubs.

Connie, who'd hitched a ride with Earl to the Brighton Valley bus depot, had purchased a ticket to downtown Houston. Once there, she took a cab to 24812 Aviary Point, which was located in a gated subdivision of large, luxurious homes, each one decorated with elaborate and tasteful lights and holiday ornaments.

After providing her ID to the guard, Connie was allowed entrance. And now, as the cab turned around in the circular drive, she stood at the front door, the baby's carrier in one hand and a single suitcase in the other. She had to place the bag on the stoop in order to ring the bell.

She could have used her key to let herself in, but decided she'd been away too long to walk in unannounced.

Elaine Harrison, her mom's personal assistant, answered the door, and Connie greeted her with a smile.

"Come on in," Elaine said. "Your mother is expecting you. She's in the den, wrapping a few last-minute presents."

As the forty-something woman reached for Connie's luggage,

she glanced down at the infant seat, where Amanda rested, her big brown eyes bright and alert.

"What a cutie pie," Elaine said, as she snatched the suitcase and straightened. "Are you babysitting?"

Connie didn't bother answering. "Is it okay if I go into the den and talk to my mom?"

Before Elaine could respond, Dinah Rawlings swept into the room, dressed to the nines as usual.

"Oh, good. You're here! I'm glad you made it for Christmas…" Dinah's comments faded into the air as her gaze lit upon Amanda. "Whose baby is that?"

"It's mine."

"Yours?" Her mother's voice bore her shock, and her brow furrowed.

Elaine cleared her throat. "Would you like me to leave you two alone? I have some work I can do in the office."

"That's probably a good idea," Dinah said. "Thank you."

After Elaine left the room, Connie said, "I've made a lot of mistakes in the past, and I'm sorry about that. But I don't count this baby as one of them. She's my biggest blessing. And you can either accept us as we are or not at all."

"Who said anything about not accepting you?" Dinah stepped closer. "You're my daughter, Connie. And that baby is my grandchild. It's just that this might take me a bit of time to get used to. I didn't even know you were pregnant."

"No one did. Not even her father." Connie bit her bottom lip, prepared for her mother's disappointment. For lectures about the importance of ratings.

"I don't understand." Dinah furrowed her brow.

"It's a long story," Connie admitted. "Let's just say I didn't want to be an embarrassment to you."

"I wish I could say thank you for the consideration, but I…" Dinah, who always held herself in check, seemed to slump a bit. "Well, I'm just so flabbergasted I don't know what to say." She glanced at Amanda again and eased closer yet. "She looks so much like your father. Can I hold her?"

"Of course." A sense of relief settled over Connie, as she set the carrier down and released Amanda from the straps that held her secure. Then she kissed her daughter's cheek before passing her to her grandmother.

Dinah took the child and held her stiffly at first, as though she'd forgotten how to hold a little one. Then, she began to soften, as it all seemed to come back to her. She marveled over her perfection, just as Connie had done that very first day, when Greg had wrapped Amanda in a flannel receiving blanket and laid her in Connie's arms.

"Just look at you." Dinah carried the baby to the sofa and took a seat. "I can see your mommy in you, too. Aren't you a precious little thing?"

When Dinah looked up, her gaze zeroed in on Connie's. Her brow, which appeared to be permanently furrowed now, twitched as she undoubtedly did a mental count of the passing months. "You said her father doesn't know about her. Why not? And who is he?"

Connie hated to admit the truth, but she owed it to her mother. And, if she had to worry about Ross finding her, she wanted her mother's support and understanding. So she took a seat beside her mom and started at the beginning, telling her about the relationship that had blown up in her face and how Ross had turned violent when he drank.

"I never could understand what you saw in him," Dinah said.

Connie took a deep breath, then shared her deepest secret, her deepest hurt. "I was lonely, Mom. Lonely for a mother and a sister, both of whom were too busy building a career and catering to an audience of viewers to care about me."

"I cared about you," Dinah countered. "Deeply. And you were never left alone."

"No, but I may as well have been. I've come to grips with it now, but at the time, I used to lock myself in my room and cry." Connie blew out a sigh, then leaned back in her seat. "Why do you think I rebelled? I just wanted some of your time and attention."

"I didn't know," Dinah said sadly. "I wish you would have said something."

"At the time, I was just a kid. I thought that, as my mother, you should have been able to figure it out. But now that I'm older, I realize that you weren't perfect, even if it was important for your viewers to think you were."

Dinah opened her mouth to say something—to argue? To object?—but the doorbell rang, interrupting their conversation.

How typical. There was always something that prevented Dinah from hearing Connie out.

"I don't have any idea who that could be." She stood, handed the baby back to Connie, then went to the door. "Well, I'll be darned. I didn't realize you'd left a friend in the car."

A friend? Connie, who held Amanda against her chest, glanced over her shoulder to see Greg on the stoop wearing jeans, a T-shirt, a leather jacket and an awkward smile. At the sight of him, her heart exploded in her chest.

What was he doing here?

She stood and made her way to the door, holding Amanda to her breast as though her love for the child could shield her from more heartbreak.

As their gazes met, he seemed…relieved to see her.

"I came to take you home," he said.

Dinah crossed her arms and glanced from one to the other.

"How did you find me?" Connie gently rocked the baby against her chest.

"It wasn't that hard. I have friends in all the right places."

"You two aren't together?" Dinah asked. "How did you get in the gate?"

"The guard is a country fan, so it only cost me an autograph." Greg shrugged a single shoulder, and a boyish grin tugged at his lips. "He also saw that damn video, and when he realized I was coming after you to tell you that I loved you, he let me in."

He came to tell her he loved her?

The pieces of her heart fluttered as though they could all go back in place—if he meant what he said.

She was both heartened and leery. Was this just another ploy to sweet-talk her into doing what he wanted?

Dinah invited Greg inside and offered him a seat.

He thanked her but remained standing. "Connie, I swear I didn't know anything about that recording. That was all Gerald's idea and it was done without my knowledge or approval. But I do admit to wanting to get you onstage. And while I'm sorry about putting you on the spot, I'm not at all sorry for singing those words from my heart. I love you, Connie. And I'll do whatever it takes to make you love me back."

"Loving you back is easy," she said. "It's finding a compromise and making a relationship work that's the hard thing. I want to create a stable home for my daughter."

"She's my daughter, too." His voice bowed with the weight of emotion. "Or close enough. I brought her into the world with you, and there's nothing I wouldn't do for her."

"Can you give her a full-time daddy?" Connie asked.

"No. But I can cut way back on my tours. And I'll take you two on whichever ones you choose."

A flood of heat spread along Connie's chest and tummy, and it took her a few beats to realize the baby had soaked through her diaper. "Uh-oh." She lifted Amanda away from her chest, only to reveal a big wet spot. She blew out a sigh. "It was a long ride from the ranch, and I guess she sprung a leak."

Greg reached for the baby. "I'll change her for you. Where's the diaper bag?"

"It's over there." Connie nodded toward the overstuffed chintz chair, where she'd left it.

As Greg carried Amanda across the room, Connie noticed an awestruck Dinah, arms crossed, a single brow arched.

"What?" Connie asked her mom.

"Your father was a jewel, honey. But he never went so far as to change diapers."

Greg had been doing a lot more than that.

Connie's thoughts drifted to the stormy night he'd delivered Amanda, the night he'd cut her cord, cleaned her up and held her for the very first time, in awe at the miracle he'd witnessed.

Her heart, which already belonged to Greg, had swelled to the bursting point as she watched him care for the baby as though she were his very own flesh and blood.

"Is there somewhere I can do this?" Greg asked Dinah.

She pointed to the guest bedroom, which was just down the hall. "It's the first door on the right."

Greg thanked her then carried Amanda and the bag into the other room.

"Anyone can be a father," Dinah said. "But it takes a very special man to be a daddy."

Connie couldn't agree more. But before she could offer a response, the bell gonged again.

In spite of the wet spot on her top, she answered only to find Ross standing there, and her heart, once warm and hopeful, chilled to the bone.

Greg, who was returning to the living room with the diaper bag slung over his shoulder, carried the baby in one arm and the wet diaper in the other. He spotted Connie at the door, talking to a long-haired man who wore a red T-shirt that revealed forearms covered with tattoos.

Greg tensed, his muscles going on instant alert.

The man, blond and fair, wore a single silver earring and an expression of remorse. "I'm sorry for hurting you, honey. It was the booze that did it. I've gone through rehab, and the band let me play with them again."

Greg didn't need an introduction to Ross, the guy who'd fathered Amanda and hit Connie. He held the baby close, wondering if he ought to pass her to Dinah so he had his hands free.

When Ross noticed Greg, recognition dawned. His gaze dropped to Amanda, and he seemed to be doing the math in his head.

"Whose baby is that?" he asked.

"She's mine," Connie admitted.

Ross's eye twitched and his jaw clenched. "Who's the father?"

Connie seemed to wrestle with the truth and a lie until her mom stepped in. "She's Greg's child. Just look at her. Anyone can see the resemblance."

Ross again gazed at Amanda, then back at Greg, who still held her close. Then he returned his focus to Connie. "When did you two…meet?"

More math, huh? It was a simple-enough deduction.

Ross's hands fisted at his sides. "If that kid is his, then that means you were screwing around on me."

Greg wanted to pound the guy senseless, but he would keep his cool—if he could. He handed the baby and the diaper to Dinah, then approached Ross. "You didn't treat her right, and she ended things with you after that last beating. So as far as I see it, our relationship is none of your business."

"But if she was living with me…"

Greg eased Connie out of the way and stood face-to-face with the man who'd hurt her. "Let me tell you what *is* your business— crossing me. She told me what you did to her, and it wouldn't take much for me to tear you limb from limb."

"That was a long time ago." Ross glanced at Connie. "The booze made me crazy."

Greg wasn't convinced that the brew was to blame, but he

didn't challenge Ross's story. "I'm glad to hear you've quit drinking, but if you so much as look at Connie or my daughter again, I'm going to file a restraining order against you. And then I'll make sure you never work for any of the major bands in the business."

"Settle down," Ross said. "I don't want any trouble."

"That's good to hear." Greg stepped back and slipped an arm around Connie, drawing her to his side. "But I don't want you falling off the wagon and then getting some wild hair and thinking you want to stake a claim on my wife."

"Your *wife?* You *married* her?"

Damn. Greg wanted to respond in a flat-out lie rather than the white variety and the ones of omission that had been going on so far, but there were too many facts that could easily be uncovered.

He narrowed his eyes at Ross. "By the time you get your car turned around and headed out of this neighborhood, we'll have the date and time set. Whatever you had with Connie before is over. Do you understand?"

"Yeah. I get it." Ross made one last effort to stand tall, to lift his chin and save his dignity. But as far as Greg was concerned, he lost every bit of self-respect the day he raised a hand in anger to Connie.

After he turned and walked away, Connie closed the door behind her. "Thank you, Greg."

He wanted to sweep her into his arms and tell her how much he loved her, how badly he wanted to let the guy have it. Instead, he said, "I meant every word I told him. I want you to be my wife, and Amanda to be my daughter. We'll be that family you want her to have."

"You have no idea how happy that makes me. I'd like nothing more than to be your wife and to create a family with you. But what about your tours? Your fans? You can't give it all up. I won't let you."

"Nothing means more to me than you and Amanda. I'm not sure how we'll work it out, honey, but we will."

"I want to believe you."

He cupped her cheeks and brushed a kiss across her brow. "Then believe it. When I set my mind to something, I make it happen."

Connie's smile lit her face, and her faith in him was staggering.

He turned to Dinah. "You need to file a complaint against that guard at the gate. It was one thing for me to slip past him, but he never should have let Ross in here."

"I'm afraid I never got around to taking his name off the list of approved guests that I have on file at the gate. I'd put him on it when he and Connie were dating. But now that I know he has a violent streak, you can be sure that I'll have him removed immediately."

Greg nodded, then watched as she called the neighborhood security office. When it was done, when Ross had been specifically eliminated, he wrapped Connie in a warm embrace. "God, it feels good to hold you again."

She smiled up at him, turning his heart on end. "I love you—more than you'll ever know."

With that, he kissed her deeply, thoroughly, claiming her as his own.

When they came up for air, he addressed Dinah. "I'd like to request your daughter's hand in marriage. And I don't want to wait any longer than it takes to get a license."

Dinah grinned and pressed a kiss on the baby's head. "If you're as much like her papa as I think you are, she's going to be a very happy woman."

Greg kissed Connie's cheek, then led her to the chair that rested beside her mother's Christmas tree, a monstrous holiday display that appeared to have been decorated by a professional.

"Sit down," he told her. "I've got a Christmas present for you."

"But we still have another day…"

"This can't wait." Greg reached into the pocket of his leather jacket and withdrew the small turquoise box tied with white satin ribbon.

"What's this?" she asked.

"Open it and see."

She untied the bow, then lifted the lid. Inside was another small box.

When she opened it, when she saw the three carat diamond, she gasped, her eyes widened in surprise. "Greg, it's beautiful."

"So are you." For a moment, it was just the two of them, caught up in a rush of emotion and promise.

But they weren't alone.

He glanced again at Dinah, who had tears welling in her eyes.

"If you two are really going to get married," she said, "I have a lot to do."

"You'll have to do it quickly." Greg tossed her a smile. "I want to be married before New Year's Eve."

Dinah's eyes widened. "But that's next week. You have no idea how much will need to be done."

"Then we'll just have to do it. One way or another, I want to start the new year as husband and wife."

Connie held up her hand and studied the sizable rock. "This is so big. You really didn't need to—"

"I *wanted* to."

Greg knew without a doubt that everything was going to be okay. That he and Connie would work things out.

"For what it's worth," Connie added, "I think we ought to record that song together."

"Oh, yeah?" Greg grinned, glad she'd finally seen it his way. Not that he'd ever force her hand again. He'd nearly lost her over it, and he wouldn't risk that again.

"And I want to sing it at our own wedding—instead of saying standard vows."

Greg's heart warmed, and he couldn't help glancing heavenward, wondering if his mother Maria was looking down on him, if she knew that he'd finally made it.

Yes, he decided.

She knew.

Then he wrapped his arms around Connie and kissed her once again—a kiss that promised a new year, a new love and a new life.

Epilogue

Two wonderful, blissful years had passed since that Christmas Eve when Greg had proposed and Connie had accepted.

One week after their engagement on New Year's Eve, they were married in a small wedding at the Rocking C Ranch with both families in attendance.

As Greg prepared to go on the winter tour, Connie announced that she and the baby would be joining him. She couldn't imagine being without her husband for that much time.

The next few months had been both hectic and tiring, but she hadn't been sorry in the least for her decision. Greg had made sure that she and the baby had as much of his free time as possible.

Then, true to his word, Greg had whittled down his schedule of concerts and had spent as much time as he could at their new home in Houston.

Still, his fame and his fan base had grown by leaps and bounds—mostly because of the song he'd recorded with Connie.

And for the past year and a half, Greg, Connie and the baby had become regulars on Dinah's holiday shows. In fact, there were plans in the making for a second Cinco de Mayo special this coming year that would be taped in the kitchen of Greg and Connie's sprawling, six-bedroom house in the Woodlands.

With Greg's praise and encouragement, Connie had developed her own spin on Tex-Mex cuisine, which had really appealed to the audience last May.

Connie's life was full, yet there was always time for walks to the park to feed the ducks, for stories before nap time and for quiet, romantic evenings with her husband.

Last night, she and Greg and the baby had spent Christmas Eve with her mother. There they'd joined Becky and her new beau, one of the musicians in Greg's band.

Connie's mom had gone to great lengths to make amends to their mother/daughter relationship. And if Connie had ever had any concerns about the kind of grandmother Dinah would be, or the time she would spend with the baby, they'd quickly disappeared once Dinah had met Amanda.

Now, as the Claytons gathered around the ten-foot Christmas tree in the living room at the Rocking C, Connie surveyed her growing family.

Nine-year-old Joey, Sabrina's nephew, was here with his father, Carlos, his new stepmother and her two young daughters. The kids were dressed in their holiday best, their eyes lit with anticipation as Jared prepared to pass out the gifts.

Two-year-old Amanda, who wore a classic red velvet dress

with satin ribbons, toddled up to Michael, Jared and Sabrina's ten-month-old son, as he held fast to the edge of the coffee table and reached for a present that sat within his reach.

In the blink of an eye, the baby tore off the gold bow and poked it into his mouth.

But his mommy was right on it.

Sabrina took the bow away and scooped him into her arms, in spite of his boisterous protest. "Come on, Mikey. Let's get your teether so you can chew on that instead."

"I'll get it, honey." Jared left his post by the tree and took off, looking for their diaper bag.

"That's going to be us next year," Matt said, as he stood behind his pregnant wife and wrapped his arms around her tummy. "Rocking babies, singing lullabies and chasing after teethers."

Connie had just begun to ponder Matt's use of plurals when Tori turned to her husband and grinned. "You've practically let the cat out of the bag anyway, honey. Let's give your mom her present now."

Granny, who was two years into her eighties, hadn't slowed down in the least. She sat up in her seat on the sofa, her ears as alert as they'd ever been. "What do you mean by that? What cat?"

Connie wasn't quite following it, either. Tori's pregnancy wasn't a surprise, especially since she'd gotten so big so quickly. She and Matt couldn't have kept it a secret if they'd tried.

"We're having twins," Matt said, a happy grin stretching across his face and lighting his eyes. "A boy and a girl."

"Well, bless my soul." Granny clapped her hands together, then kept them clasped. "Ask and you shall receive."

"But we didn't *ask* for twins," Tori said, her eyes glimmering and her face glowing.

"I'm the one who asked." Granny chuckled, and a sly grin formed. "At my age, I thought the good Lord might want to start blessing me with grandbabies two at a time."

Everyone laughed, and Connie turned to Greg. "Should we share our news now, too?"

The grin that crinkled Greg's eyes stretched across his face, and he nodded. "I think this is the perfect time and place for an announcement."

Connie faced her new family. "Greg and I will be having another baby next summer."

"Whoo-hoo!" Granny got to her feet and looked from Sabrina to Jared and back to Sabrina. "Three new babies. Anyone want to make that four?"

The couple laughed, and Jared said, "We were actually talking about that this morning, Granny. And since we'd like to have our kids close in age, we're going to give that some serious consideration in the coming months."

As Connie scanned the room and looked at her new family, her heart filled with contentment. What a blessing it was to be a part of the Clayton clan.

And so was being married to Greg—her best friend, her lover, her partner for life.

Greg must have been having the same thoughts as she was, because he wrapped her in a warm embrace. "Merry Christmas, honey."

Connie's joy was impossible to contain. "Merry Christmas to you, too."

"Each December gets better and better," he said. "Don't you think?"

"Yes I do." And she couldn't be happier.

To prove it, she kissed her husband and the father of her babies with all the love in her heart.

* * * * *

Silhouette Desire kicks off 2009 with
MAN OF THE MONTH, *a yearlong program*
featuring incredible heroes by stellar authors.

When Navy SEAL Hunter Cabot returns home for some
much-needed R & R, he discovers he's a married man.
There's just one problem: he's never met his "bride."

Enjoy this sneak peek at Maureen Child's
AN OFFICER AND A MILLIONAIRE.
Available January 2009 from Silhouette Desire.

One

Hunter Cabot, Navy SEAL, had a healing bullet wound in his side, thirty days' leave and, apparently, a wife he'd never met.

On the drive into his hometown of Springville, California, he stopped for gas at Charlie Evans's service station. That's where the trouble started.

"Hunter! Man, it's good to see you! Margie didn't tell us you were coming home."

"Margie?" Hunter leaned back against the front fender of his black pickup truck and winced as his side gave a small twinge of pain. Silently then, he watched as the man he'd known since high school filled his tank.

Charlie grinned, shook his head and pumped gas. "Guess your wife was lookin' for a little 'alone' time with you, huh?"

"My—" Hunter couldn't even say the word. *Wife?* He didn't have a wife. "Look, Charlie..."

"Don't blame her, of course," his friend said with a wink as he finished up and put the gas cap back on. "You being gone all the time with the SEALs must be hard on the ol' love life."

He'd never had any complaints, Hunter thought, frowning at the man still talking a mile a minute. "What're you—"

"Bet Margie's anxious to see you. She told us all about that R & R trip you two took to Bali." Charlie's dark brown eyebrows lifted and wiggled.

"Charlie..."

"Hey, it's okay, you don't have to say a thing, man."

What the hell could he say? Hunter shook his head, paid for his gas and as he left, told himself Charlie was just losing it. Maybe the guy had been smelling gas fumes too long.

But as it turned out, it wasn't just Charlie. Stopped at a red light on Main Street, Hunter glanced out his window to smile at Mrs. Harker, his second-grade teacher who was now at least a hundred years old. In the middle of the crosswalk, the old lady stopped and shouted, "Hunter Cabot, you've got yourself a wonderful wife. I hope you appreciate her."

Scowling now, he only nodded at the old woman—the only teacher who'd ever scared the crap out of him. What the hell was going on here? Was everyone but him nuts?

His temper beginning to boil, he put up with a few more comments about his "wife" on the drive through town before finally pulling into the wide, circular drive leading to the Cabot mansion. Hunter didn't have a clue what was going on, but he planned to get to the bottom of it. Fast.

He grabbed his duffel bag, stalked into the house and paid no attention to the housekeeper, who ran at him, fluttering both hands. "Mr. Hunter!"

"Sorry, Sophie," he called out over his shoulder as he took the stairs two at a time. "Need a shower, then we'll talk."

He marched down the long, carpeted hallway to the rooms that were always kept ready for him. In his suite, Hunter tossed the duffel down and stopped dead. The shower in his bathroom was running. His *wife?*

Anger and curiosity boiled in his gut, creating a churning mass that had him moving forward without even thinking about it. He opened the bathroom door to a wall of steam and the sound of a woman singing—off-key. Margie, no doubt.

Well, if she was his wife... Hunter walked across the room, yanked the shower door open and stared in at a curvy, naked, temptingly wet woman.

She whirled to face him, slapping her arms across her naked body while she gave a short, terrified scream.

Hunter smiled. "Hi, honey. I'm home."

* * * * *

Be sure to look for
AN OFFICER AND A MILLIONAIRE
by USA TODAY *bestselling author Maureen Child.*
Available January 2009 from Silhouette Desire.

You're invited to join our Tell Harlequin Reader Panel!

By joining our new reader panel you will:

- Receive Harlequin® books—they are FREE and yours to keep with no obligation to purchase anything!
- Participate in fun online surveys
- Exchange opinions and ideas with women just like you
- Have a say in our new book ideas and help us publish the best in women's fiction

In addition, you will have a chance to win great prizes and receive special gifts! See Web site for details. Some conditions apply. Space is limited.

To join, visit us at

www.TellHarlequin.com.

New York Times **Bestselling Author**

SHERRYL WOODS

When Jeanette Brioche helped to launch The Corner Spa, she found more than professional satisfaction—she discovered deep friendships. But even the Sweet Magnolias can't persuade her that the holidays are anything more than misery.

Pushed into working on the town's Christmas festival, Jeanette teams up with the sexy new town manager. Tom McDonald may be the only person in Serenity who's less enthused about family and the holidays than she is.

But with romance in the air, Jeanette and Tom discover that this just may be a season of miracles, after all.

Welcome to Serenity

The Sweet Magnolias

Available the first week of December 2008 wherever paperbacks are sold!

REQUEST YOUR FREE BOOKS!

2 FREE NOVELS PLUS 2 FREE GIFTS!

Silhouette®

SPECIAL EDITION®

Life, Love and Family!

YES! Please send me 2 FREE Silhouette Special Edition® novels and my 2 FREE gifts (gifts are worth about $10). After receiving them, if I don't wish to receive any more books, I can return the shipping statement marked "cancel." If I don't cancel, I will receive 6 brand-new novels every month and be billed just $4.24 per book in the U.S. or $4.99 per book in Canada, plus 25¢ shipping and handling per book and applicable taxes, if any*. That's a savings of at least 15% off the cover price! I understand that accepting the 2 free books and gifts places me under no obligation to buy anything. I can always return a shipment and cancel at any time. Even if I never buy another book from Silhouette, the two free books and gifts are mine to keep forever.

235 SDN EEYU   335 SDN EEY6

Name	(PLEASE PRINT)

Address	Apt. #

City	State/Prov.	Zip/Postal Code

Signature (if under 18, a parent or guardian must sign)

Mail to the Silhouette Reader Service:

IN U.S.A.: P.O. Box 1867, Buffalo, NY 14240-1867
IN CANADA: P.O. Box 609, Fort Erie, Ontario L2A 5X3

Not valid to current subscribers of Silhouette Special Edition books.

Want to try two free books from another line?
Call 1-800-873-8635 or visit www.morefreebooks.com.

* Terms and prices subject to change without notice. N.Y. residents add applicable sales tax. Canadian residents will be charged applicable provincial taxes and GST. Offer not valid in Quebec. This offer is limited to one order per household. All orders subject to approval. Credit or debit balances in a customer's account(s) may be offset by any other outstanding balance owed by or to the customer. Please allow 4 to 6 weeks for delivery. Offer available while quantities last.

Your Privacy: Silhouette is committed to protecting your privacy. Our Privacy Policy is available online at www.eHarlequin.com or upon request from the Reader Service. From time to time we make our lists of customers available to reputable third parties who may have a product or service of interest to you. If you would prefer we not share your name and address, please check here. ☐

SSE08R

Inside ROMANCE

Stay up-to-date on all your romance reading news!

The Inside Romance newsletter is a FREE quarterly newsletter highlighting our upcoming series releases and promotions!

Click on the <u>Inside Romance</u> link on the front page of **www.eHarlequin.com** or e-mail us at insideromance@harlequin.ca to sign up to receive your FREE newsletter today!

You can also subscribe by writing us at: HARLEQUIN BOOKS Attention: Customer Service Department P.O. Box 9057, Buffalo, NY 14269-9057

Please allow 4-6 weeks for delivery of the first issue by mail.

COMING NEXT MONTH